Endorsements for the *Love Blossoms in Oregon* Series

Wishing on Buttercups

"A family tragedy, a woman scarred for life, a chance meeting, and a charming ensemble cast blend together to make Miralee Ferrell's Wishing on Buttercups a story that runs the gamut of emotions from enthralling to heart-wrenching, to the enjoyable, satisfying end."

Vickie McDonough, award-winning author of the Pioneer Promises series

Blowing on Dandelions

"*Blowing on Dandelions* is an amazing, deeply emotional story. Each of the characters is so sympathetic and well drawn that it was impossible to put the book down. Ferrell is a wonderful writer who handles the pain of physical and emotional trauma beautifully. Her characters are appealing, with a touching and believable faith journey, and the romance is lovely. My only regret was reaching the final page! Miralee Ferrell's future books will be an automatic purchase from now on!"

Roxanne Rustand, author of *Duty to Protect*

"In *Blowing on Dandelions*, Miralee Ferrell gives us an engaging story with strong characters who have hidden depths. The theme of the story is universal and will touch hearts and help heal longtime hurts. As with all of her books, Miralee weaves a satisfying romance through these pages. What else could a reader ask for?"

Lena Nelson Dooley, speaker and author of the 2012 Selah Award winner *Maggie's Journey, Mary's Blessing* and the 2011 Will Rogers Medallion Award winner *Love Finds You in Golden, New Mexico*

"In *Blowing on Dandelions*, Miralee Ferrell has an excellent way of keeping the words flowing, keeping the reader following, and investing in the characters. I particularly love the redemption she shows, where not all offensive people are evil, but merely hurting. Of course, the love story makes for a perfectly satisfying ending. Very well done!"

Hannah Alexander, award-winning author of the Hideaway Series

"Miralee Ferrell's *Blowing on Dandelions* is a deeply inspiring story about family conflict and the transforming power of rekindled love. A richly written story chock full of nuggets of divine wisdom, this book was, for me, a genuinely satisfying read."

Walt Larimore, best-selling author of *Hazel Creek* and *Sugar Fork*

Forget Me Not

Love Blossoms in Oregon Series

Blowing on Dandelions

Forget Me Not—Novella

Wishing on Buttercups

Dreaming on Daisies

MIRALEE
FERRELL

A Novel

Forget Me Not

Love Blossoms in Oregon

Mountain
Brook
Ink

FORGET ME NOT
Published by Mountain Brook Ink
White Salmon, WA 98672

This story is a work of fiction. All characters and events are the product of the author's imagination. Any resemblance to any person, living or dead, is coincidental.

Scripture quotations are taken from the King James Version of the Bible. Public domain.

Published by Mountain Brook INK
Miralee Ferrell, Christy Caughie, Gilded Heart Design, Kim Bowman, and Susan Marlow—formatting
Cover Art: Christy Caughie, Gilded Heart Design

Printed in the United States of America
First Edition 2014

1 2 3 4 5 6 7 8 9 10 11 12 13 14

To Brian and Hannah—I'm so thankful God sent me
such an awesome son-in-law and daughter-in-law. You
are both a blessing to our family.

Psalm 103:2
Bless the LORD, O my soul, And forget not all His
benefits:

Psalm 119:16
I will delight myself in Your statutes; I will
not forget Your word.

Acknowledgments

This is my first self-published novel, or novella, as it were, and it's been quite a learning experience. First, I must thank the wonderful people at David C Cook Publishing for encouraging me to write this novella and allowing me to tie it into my *Love Blossoms in Oregon* series. They published the first two books in that series, as well as the third, *Dreaming on Daisies*, releasing October 1, 2014. My marketing director, Karen Stoller, and my publisher, Don Pape (whom I named a character after in book 3) were both helpful and encouraging, and I appreciate them so much.

My brother, Tim Gould, gave me helpful suggestions on how to get my feet wet in the world of Indie publishing. Margaret Daley, Cheryl Hodde (Hannah Alexander), Carrie Turansky, Virginia Smith and Mary DeMuth all provided valuable insight into the Indie world and helped me make wise choices. Thank you all!

I was so blessed to discover Christy Caughie, a talented graphic designer and owner of *Gilded Heart Design*, who put together my amazing cover. She and I worked on it together, but it was her vision and gift that made it come to life. I can't thank Christy enough for her work and creativity. A close friend and fellow author, Susan Marlow, did the formatting for my print book, and I can't thank her enough.

My wonderful critique group offered suggestions and edits, and as always, I couldn't do it without you. Thank you, Kimberly Rose Johnson, Margaret Daley and Vickie

McDonough. You girls rock! I want to acknowledge a team of advance readers who offered wonderful input—in fact, two new scenes were written due to suggestions by Ramisa, as well as helpful edits by Judy V., Linda L., and Sylvia.

Then there's my Street Team—Barbara, Britney, Carole, Deborah, Diana, Iris, Janice, Jennie, Judy C., Judy V., Linda, Liz, Melissa, Nancee, Sarah and Sarah, Shelly, Teresa K., Teresa M., Tonya, and Wanda who worked so hard to pass the word to readers.

These ladies work tirelessly on my behalf, and they offered insight and suggestions as we put the cover together for *Forget Me Not*. I'm so thankful for their brainstorming, advance reading and general marketing help these ladies give me as I go through the process.

As always, I can't thank my family enough—they bear with me through the deadlines, edits, the publicity push, the stress-filled days when I question whether I should really be writing—and they make it all worthwhile. I love you all.

To my readers who have remained faithful through all my books, and to those who are just now discovering my work—thank you. If it weren't for you, I wouldn't keep writing. If you haven't read *Blowing on Dandelions* yet, or *Wishing on Buttercups*, I hope you'll do so soon. You'll meet an entire cast of characters—and some of them truly are 'characters'—that I believe you'll come to love as much as I do. I purposely remained vague about certain people and details so I wouldn't ruin anything for those of you who haven't read either two or three. However, you would do well to read book 1, if possible, to meet the folks who people this series, and learn their stories.

And most importantly, I thank my Lord and Savior, Jesus Christ, with whom all things are possible and all things are brought into being. He gave me the creativity to write and called me to this career path, which I also see as a ministry, and I'll continue on as long as He asks me to.

I value every email I receive, as well as the posts on Facebook, Twitter, Goodreads, and Pinterest, and I'd love to have you drop by. Thank you for your faithful support!

Chapter One

Baker City, Oregon
Early Summer, 1881

Julia McKenzie slipped out the back door of the Baker City Saloon and peered down the alley, willing her heart to quit racing. Her breath came in short spurts, and she wiped her clammy hands down the sides of her full skirt. Wagons, and men on horseback, moved past the far end where the alley opened on Front Street, but no one looked her way.

Dark clouds obscured the sun, creating deep shadows in the crevices of the narrow space running between the long rows of businesses.

She stepped into the middle of the alley, her spine straight. She'd done nothing to be ashamed of, even if the respectable people in this town might not agree. A cheery whistle emanating from a short distance alerted her but not in time to fade out of sight.

A tall man strode toward her, his face shadowed by his hat and the dim light that filtered into this narrow space between the dingy buildings. He slowed as he approached and tipped his hat. "Are you lost, ma'am?"

Pivoting a half-turn, he glanced over his shoulder then at her. "Is your husband nearby?"

Julia lifted her chin. The man's voice niggled at her memory, but she couldn't quite place it. "I'm not lost, but thank you for asking." She knew what would come next. The sly smile, the knowing look at the saloon door only paces away, then the suggestive remark. Sometimes following her calling was almost more than she could bear.

He nodded and swept off his hat, revealing dark, short-cropped curls. "May I escort you to where you're going, then?" He replaced his hat then held out his arm. A gentle smile warmed his features, barely discernible under the brim.

She retreated a half-step. "Why?" She crossed her arms over her chest. "I'll have you know I'm not that kind of woman. I won't go to your home or to a hotel room, if that's what you have in mind."

He winced and lowered his arm. "I'm sorry. Maybe I should introduce myself. I'm the pastor of Baker City Community Church. I simply felt it wasn't safe for you to walk through this section of town alone."

Her body gave an involuntary jerk, and warmth rushed to her cheeks. Of all the people in this town she could bump into behind a saloon, it had to be a preacher!

Seth Russell tried not to stare at the striking woman standing an arm's length from him. This cramped space didn't allow for good visibility, but through glints of sunlight he noted rich, upswept auburn hair, delicate lips set in an oval face, and sapphire eyes opened wide in apparent surprise. He glimpsed incredible feeling shining from their depths as the clouds drifted away from the face of the sun. Then resentment and indignation followed with a flash of shock and—what? Fear? Guilt? Or something else he couldn't quite comprehend.

But there was something more. He knew this woman—he was certain of it. Much had passed between now and the last time he'd seen her, but his heart rate increased, almost threatening to choke him. He knew it was true. Julia McKenzie. Would she recognize him?

"I apologize, Pastor." Her well-modulate voice roused him from contemplation. "I assumed—"

He held up his hand. "No need to explain. I know what some of the men hereabouts are like, especially in this area. In fact, I suggest we don't linger, or we may draw undesirable attention." He held out his arm again and waited for several long heartbeats. Once they stepped out of the alley and into better light, would she realize who accompanied her? And what was she doing in this rough part of town without an escort and so close to the saloon? The last thing he wanted to do was embarrass her, but they'd left too many things unspoken, those seven years ago.

She moved with a quiet grace and slipped her hand under the crook of his elbow. "Thank you. My name is Julia McKenzie. I was here—" She shook her head. "It doesn't matter why. I'm sorry to trouble you. If you care to accompany me to the Arlington Hotel, I'd be most grateful."

Seth pressed her hand against his side, not wanting her to slip away or possibly stumble over the refuse in the alley. "Julia." He barely breathed the name then bit back the rest of what he'd planned to say. Seth hoped she hadn't heard—it wasn't the right time—but he could barely contain his excitement.

He steered her around a particularly disgusting pile of rotted food and discarded trash tossed from the door of another less-than-reputable establishment.

He hazarded a quick glance at the young woman—Julia McKenzie, whatever else she might have become, was even lovelier than she'd been all those years ago. She wasn't dressed like someone who worked at a saloon or any other business in this part of town, but what else could have brought her? "Miss McKenzie?"

Her gaze flitted past his, but he saw no recognition. "Yes?"

"Are you new to town? It's easy to lose your way if you aren't familiar with the streets."

A small smile dimpled her cheeks. "I've been here for three weeks or so. And no, I wasn't lost." Her lips pressed together after the last word as though afraid something more would slip out.

Seth nodded but kept his own counsel. It wasn't his nature to pry, although he'd like to help if there was a need—and he most certainly wanted to know where this woman had been for the past seven years. "Might I invite you to church this Sunday, if you aren't already attending somewhere?"

He paused at the mouth of the alley, allowing his vision to adjust to the brighter sunlight. A group of rough-clad men bunched around the front door of the saloon a stone's throw to his left, and the wheels of a wagon, heavily laden with boxes and bags, churned a cloud of dust as it passed. "Let's walk this way." He drew her to the side, apart from the gawking men, and waited for her to step onto the boardwalk beside him.

"I'm not sure if I'll attend, but I'll consider it. Thank you." Her quiet words surprised him, but she kept her face averted, never looking at him squarely. Was she afraid of something? How could he find out more about her without being direct? But with all they'd been to one another in the past, perhaps he should simply be forthright.

"Do you know where my church is located? I'm afraid it's a bit of a walk from your hotel. I could ask the Jacobs family to stop by on their way."

"No." The word was quick and almost sharp. "Thank you. I don't care to be a bother." She flicked her fingers toward an open door a few yards down the boardwalk. "I appreciate you walking with me, Pastor. We're here."

He slowed his stride and came to a halt as her hand slipped from his arm, then he deliberately turned to face her. "I'd appreciate if you'd call me Seth as you used to do. I see you don't recognize me after all these years. Of course, I'm clean shaven, my hair is much shorter and I'm several years older. I decided the full beard didn't suit me. I'm Seth Russell. It's been a long time, Julia."

Her gaze swung to his and clung, and she seemed almost to have quit breathing. "Seth—Russell?"

He nodded but didn't speak, wanting to give her time to absorb the information.

She placed the tips of her fingers against her lips. "Oh my. I didn't realize—forgive me for not knowing you sooner."

"It's been seven years, and I suppose we've both changed."

Julia's head dipped slightly in acknowledgment. "Yes." The word was a mere whisper. "I didn't know you'd gone into the ministry. As I recall, you were headed a different direction when we . . ." She caught her bottom lip between her teeth and looked away.

"When we began courting. Yes. I had a change of heart not long after you left." Seth felt as though he'd choke over the last three words, but he'd forced them out. He hadn't spoken to Julia for years, although he'd never forgotten her, and his heart had yet to recover. "What brought you to Baker City? And more importantly, why did you leave Omaha and not speak to me personally?"

Julia didn't reply. Her fingers moved, and it appeared she might touch him, but she halted. "I'm so sorry, Seth." She pivoted and moved with deliberate steps toward the hotel.

Disquiet and loss slammed into Seth as she disappeared. He longed to follow and discover more, but he forced himself to retreat. He might be a pastor who cared for his flock, and even more important, a man she'd once acted as though she cared for—but she'd made it clear she had no desire to share her personal business. What or who she might be now was not his concern. But that didn't stop anticipation from spreading through his veins at the thought of possibly seeing her again on Sunday.

Julia stood just inside the hotel foyer and waited until Seth turned the corner at the end of the street and disappeared from view. Placing her palm over her pounding heart, she willed it to calm and slow.

Never in a thousand years had she expected to meet Seth in Baker City. The last thing she'd heard, he'd gone west—although truth-be-told, she'd heard he'd headed to Oregon. Had she secretly hoped to find him here when she'd made her decision to come?

She should have recognized him the moment she laid eyes on him, but he'd introduced himself as a pastor before speaking his name. He had matured into a handsome, rugged man, quite different from the youth she'd known so many years ago.

As soon as she'd heard his voice, she'd experienced a rush of awareness that had almost overpowered her, but she'd pushed it away as ridiculous. The Seth Russell she'd known had been reckless and bold—certainly not someone she believed would ever become a pastor. In fact, that independent spirit was what drew her to him in the beginning

Papa had expressed reservations because Seth was an orphan with no proper upbringing or family to help keep him on the straight and narrow. Julia shook her head in wonder. Her father had worried Seth would do something foolish or go the wrong direction—and here he'd ended up as a pastor—just like Papa.

On the other hand, Seth had hinted at some kind of life change not long before she'd walked out of his life. Looking back, she knew she'd been a coward. At the very least, she should have talked to Seth and explained, not simply sent him a letter. She'd cared for him more than any man she'd ever known, but she'd only been seventeen and not ready to commit herself—in fact, the thought of marriage scared her.

At four years her senior, Seth had tried more than once to declare himself. He wanted to settle down and marry, even if he was overly adventurous in other ways; but Julia had forestalled that avowal from happening.

While most young women wanted nothing more than to marry and start a family, she had desired more. She'd been raised in a sheltered family—a pastor's family, no less—and longed to spread her wings and experience life before being confined by the chains of matrimony. At least, that's how it had seemed at the time.

After seeing Seth again, Julia wasn't so sure she'd made the right choice. He'd grown into a handsome man. Not that he wasn't handsome before, but maturity sat well on him. And there was something in the depth of his gaze she'd never noticed—wisdom, perhaps?

Now she regretted letting him think she might attend his church on Sunday. Why had she been so quick to even consider his request? Part of her missed that life— the steady, secure existence she'd known growing up.

Not only that, she missed the fellowship of other believers, but Julia knew all too well the whispers that would start if people got wind of what she was doing—or that she'd known Seth in the past. She hadn't given her word, and it might be better if she didn't show up for service. But try as she might, she couldn't convince herself to stay away. She wanted to see Seth again, even if only once more.

Julia shoved down the prickles of guilt assaulting her conscience—she hadn't lied or even offered a half-truth in letting him accompany her to the hotel where she resided—she'd simply avoided saying it wasn't her final destination.

Opening the door a crack, she peered outside, then slipped into step with a family passing by. An older woman hobbled along with them, gripping the hand of the younger girl. Julia stayed close behind the pair, hoping to blend into the group.

The child tugged on the older woman's hand. "Grandma, you're limping. Ma! Grandma's feet are hurting. We need to stop and let her rest."

The blond woman, apparently the child's mother, slowed her pace and drew abreast of the pair. "Mama, do you want to find a bench and sit?"

"Nonsense, Katherine. My feet are fine, although it is most kind of Amanda to worry." She loosened her grip and smoothed the child's golden curls. "I am anxious to visit the theater and hear the concert."

Julia's heart sank. The theater was only another block, and she needed to go a distance beyond. Well, it didn't matter. Quickening her stride, she struck out around the family, peeking at the woman called Katherine. What a kind face and gentle demeanor. But no doubt that would turn to disgust if she knew Julia's plan. She had always been alone in her desires and would probably never have a friend like this woman, no matter how badly she wanted one.

She squared her shoulders. There was no room for self-pity in her life. Her mission came above all else. Her mind drifted to her impetuous response to Seth's invitation. She'd attend church one time, but that almost certainly would be the end of it. Once his congregation knew her secret business, she'd never be allowed to set foot in the building again, and no doubt Seth would feel the same.

If someone saw her venturing into an area where proper white women were rarely seen, so be it. She'd come out West to hide from wagging tongues, but if they started to wag here as well, there was nothing she could do to stop it. It was time to quit sneaking around like a thief, hoping no one would notice.

Chapter Two

Julia rapped on the flimsy wood frame of the shack. What would Seth think if he knew she was here? His expression had held a question when he'd first spotted her in the alley behind the saloon. Regardless of how kind or compassionate he might be, that would certainly change if he could see her now.

"Hallo." A young boy peeked out of the canvas door. "What you want, lady?"

"I'm looking for Lee Mei. Is she home?"

The boy's black eyes widened. "Why you want her? She in trouble?"

"No, not at all. I'm a friend. May I speak to her?"

"Meng? Who is here?" A soft voice called from inside.

"She say a friend." He swung back to Julia. "What your name, lady?"

"Julia." She doubted the boy could pronounce her last name and besides, Mei only knew her Christian name.

He patted his thin chest and grinned. "Ju-la." He nodded. "I Lee Meng. Meng mean fierce. Like tiger. I learn English from Mei."

Julia wanted to hug the boy. Mei had said that her little brother was ten, but his undernourished body looked more like that of a much younger child. "You are a good student, Meng. Your English is excellent."

He grinned, his eyes sparkling, then bowed and pushed the canvas aside. "Please to enter, nice lady."

It took a few seconds to adjust to the dim light, and Julia held still until she could see Mei lying on a pallet a short distance from the door. An old woman bent over a washtub in the far corner, humming a haunting tune while she scrubbed a white shirt across a washboard. She didn't seem to notice Julia's presence.

Julia moved to the pallet and knelt. "What's wrong? I went to the saloon to see you, but they said you hadn't come in to work." She winced, remembering the vile words that had spewed from the manager's lips as he'd answered her questions. "Are you sick?"

Meng moved to her side. "Bad man hit her. Make her cry. I tell Mei not go back there." He shook his head. "She no listen."

Mei pushed herself to an elbow and flinched. "Shh. Go help Grandmother. Carry basket outside and hang clothes." She waggled her finger at him when he hesitated. "Go now, my fierce warrior."

His face beamed, and he pivoted toward the old woman still bent over her task.

Julia leaned closer and dropped her voice to a whisper, barely able to force the words past the lump of rage lodged in her throat. "Someone hurt you? Tell me what happened and who hit you. I'll get the sheriff and have the man arrested."

Mei shrugged. "Sheriff no care. Men beat Chinese all the time." She shifted and winced. "I not want to go to work tonight. Meng took message to Crawford that I sick, but he say I come soon or lose job."

The boy hefted the basket onto his hip and pushed through the door, staggering under the weight. "Like I tell you, missy Ju-la, she no listen." He shouldered through the canvas, and silence settled over the shack.

Julia glanced at the old woman still crouched in the corner. "What does your grandmother say? Surely she doesn't want you to return. Can't you stay here and help take in more laundry?"

Mei hiked herself up against the wall and leaned back, eyelids closed. "I not tell her the truth. Grandfather die in the mines last year and father not come home for three weeks. I think he dead, too. We need money, Miss Julia. Meng need clothes and good food. Not make enough money washing for miners."

Julia clenched her jaw, certain the women were getting cheated by the men who brought their laundry. It was a common enough practice when the Chinese workers didn't have a clear understanding of American money.

Over one hundred people inhabited Chinatown, situated on the edge of Baker City, but if the mines continued to produce silver and gold, more would come. They were cheap labor and hard workers, digging ditches and cooking in the mining camps. If only the good people of this town wouldn't look down on them but would rise up and demand fair treatment.

She almost laughed at the ludicrous thought. Who was she trying to fool? The so-called Christians in this area wouldn't even allow one of Mei's people to attend a service.

Determination pushed Julia to her feet. "I'm going to try to find you a decent job. You can't keep going to that saloon. I hate it that those men handle and misuse you. Please, Mei. At least think about not returning tonight?"

The young woman smiled. "I go. You no worry. Remember, you say your God will protect me. I pray with you and trust Him. He not let me die."

Stark fear slammed Julia so hard it stole her breath as her glib words returned to haunt her. What had she been thinking, making such a rash promise? Who was she to say God would protect Mei, her family, or any of the Chinese?

No one cared about these people or their problems, and so often the authorities looked the other way. She'd heard good things about the sheriff, but more than likely he was no different than most men when it came to affairs with Mei's people.

For one heart-stopping moment an image of Mei's bruised and battered body lying in the alley clouded her vision, then she shoved the image from her mind, refusing to dwell on something she couldn't control.

"We will pray that God will send His angels to watch over you, Mei. I know He loves you, but I don't trust the men who go to the saloon. Not when they've been drinking. We still need to be careful, even when we pray. Promise me you'll be careful?"

Mei reached out and grasped Julia's hand. "Help me stand?" Her movements were slow and deliberate, but she got to her feet and straightened her spine. "You no worry. I be fine. You see."

Julia gave her a careful hug and backed toward the door. If only she could take Mei's place at her job, but that would be too much, even for her. At this point all she could do was trust the God she'd introduced Mei to and pray He truly would watch out for her, just as she'd promised.

Seth left the pulpit and strode down the aisle of his church after service finished Sunday morning. A sour taste coated his mouth at the actions of some of the members of his congregation. Julia had slipped in right before the organ played the opening hymn. She'd sat near the rear of the sanctuary, but he'd still noticed a number of heads turning. In fact, more than one matron's mouth was turned down in a frown, and he'd better find out why.

A small knot of people congregated around the young woman, and Seth only noted two friendly faces in the bunch—Katherine Jacobs and Beth Roberts, a young woman who boarded with Mrs. Jacobs.

Mrs. Horace Evans' strident voice reached his ears while he was still in motion. "Where do you live, my dear? I declare, I thought I saw you leaving Chinatown a few days ago."

Katherine touched Mrs. Evans's arm. "The streets are so congested with miners and new people to the area, I'm sure you must be mistaken. Besides, Miss McKenzie certainly has the right to walk wherever she pleases."

Beth nodded and squeezed Julia's arm, but the young woman didn't speak.

Mrs. Evans' bobbing head sent the feathers and flowers on her cumbersome hat into a wild dance. She planted a fist on her ample hip and raised an eyebrow.

"But why would Miss McKenzie be there, is what I want to know? No lady would venture into that area, Mrs. Jacobs. Surely if she had business with one of *those people*, she could send someone in with a note. That section is rife with criminals and riff-raff. A decent woman wouldn't be safe."

She shot Julia a harsh look. "And I can't for the life of me imagine any decent woman caring to be there."

Seth slowed and cleared his throat. Mrs. Thompson and Mrs. Beal scurried off, but as he'd expected, Mrs. Evans stood her ground. Katherine moved a half-step closer to Miss McKenzie, whose wide blue eyes moved from him to Mrs. Evans. The woman was once again proving true to her kind—a gossip without the slightest scruples when it came to charity.

If only he'd gotten to Julia before the older matron could voice her concerns. Although he was surprised she'd mentioned Chinatown rather than the seedier part of town where he'd met Julia a few days ago. What Julia could be doing haunting the alley behind a row of saloons as well as visiting Chinatown, he couldn't imagine.

Regardless, it was up to him to intervene and put her at ease. "Ladies, I'm sorry to interrupt, but I haven't had a chance to greet our visitor yet."

He dipped his head toward Julia, who looked ready to bolt. "Miss McKenzie, it's good to see you again. I'm happy you were able to make it to service."

As soon as the words left his lips, he wished he could retract them. Mrs. Evans' brows rose, and he could almost see her salivating over the fact that they'd already met.

"Pastor Russell." Julia nodded and smiled, but it didn't quite reach her eyes. "I enjoyed your sermon. I haven't thought about the Sermon on the Mount in quite that way before. You've given me something to consider."

Mrs. Evans sucked in a breath and opened her lips, but Katherine forestalled her. "Miss McKenzie, we're having a church gathering this evening—a potluck supper of sorts—and we'd love to have you join us."

Seth's heart jumped. He'd almost forgotten the affair but turned to Julia, hoping she'd accept. "Yes, we would. Don't feel you must bring anything."

Mrs. Evans crossed her arms and harrumphed. "Everyone brings a dish, Pastor Seth. And I'd still like to know why Miss McKenzie was visiting Chinatown. Also, how do you know her when this is her first time visiting our church?"

Seth struggled to maintain his temper. Mable Evans seemed to thrive on stirring up trouble. "We bumped into one another in town a couple of days ago. Miss McKenzie is a visitor here and should not be questioned as though she's done something wrong."

He turned to the young woman. "If you need a ride to our potluck, I'm sure we can arrange for a buggy to pick you up."

She took a step back. "Thank you, but no. I'm afraid I'm not one to get involved in social functions."

Katherine smiled. "We'd love to have you join us." She shot a look at Mrs. Evans. "And I'd like to introduce you to some of the other women I count as dear friends who will make you feel quite at home."

Julia moved closer to the exit. "I appreciate it, but I'm afraid I'm quite busy. I'll come to church when I'm able, but I can't promise more. Good-day, ladies." She nodded at Seth. "Pastor." She pivoted and walked out the door, her posture erect and navy blue skirt swishing around her ankles.

Seth stood without moving, working to swallow the lump in his throat. Julia said she was too busy to attend church regularly and didn't care to attend church functions. His thoughts darted to seven years earlier to another town and what felt like another life, and the young woman who had walked out on him.

She had loved every aspect of the social and church life and encouraged him when he'd received invitations from various city dignitaries. But the one time he'd shared his dream of ministering to the broken and wounded she'd shivered.

He'd never understood—he'd assumed she'd be happy about it, since her father was a pastor—but he'd never had a chance to tell her. She'd sent a letter ending their friendship before it could even reach the point of an engagement.

At the age of twenty-eight, he had accepted the fact he'd never marry. All the same, his heart stung as the vision in blue disappeared from sight.

Julia kept her stride even and her focus straight ahead, but she couldn't shake the disquiet that gripped her when she'd looked into Seth's warm gaze. He and Mrs. Jacobs had done all in their power to deter the obnoxious woman who'd questioned her after church.

In fact, he'd appeared quite anxious to change the subject when Mrs. Evans inquired about their previous acquaintance. Julia had quelled a grimace when Seth had inadvertently let it slip they'd met in the past, but he'd done an admirable job in steering the conversation a different direction.

Mrs. Evans had been like a horse with the bit in its teeth, determined to run away with the conversation and trample anyone who got in her way. Julia had met that kind of woman before who wanted nothing more than to poke her nose in everyone else's business.

No good could come of attending that church, but her heart longed to fit in somewhere. And not simply to fit in, but to see Seth again. Why did people have to judge things they didn't understand, simply because they saw her in a part of town that might be less desirable than others?

She stepped onto the boardwalk and headed toward her hotel, dodging the men who littered the streets. Coarse miners, well-dressed gamblers and tidy-looking businessmen could be seen, all hurrying to some destination.

How many of them slipped out from under the watchful regard of their wives or sweethearts and into the dancehall to make the acquaintance of one of the poor women who were unfortunate enough to work there?

From her experience these past few years, men were all cut from the same cloth. Except Seth—and Papa.

She smiled at the memory, wishing her father were still alive to see the work she was doing now. He'd be so happy she'd turned away from frivolous living and directed her thoughts to caring for others instead of herself.

Her steps faltered at the door to her hotel. Did she want to go sit in her room the rest of the afternoon? She'd made no real friends since arriving in this town, but then, she'd not expected to. A vision of Katherine Jacobs came to mind. Would she still offer friendship if she knew what Julia did with her spare time?

If only she dared attend the church social tonight. She sighed and pushed through the door. No doubt Mrs. Evans wasn't the only one with a sharp pair of eyes, and if she was any judge of character, the woman would be telling her tale to every person in the church who cared to listen.

The comfortable hotel lobby didn't entice her to linger this time, even though she was hungry for news of the outside world. Going to the supper tonight or even sitting in the lobby wasn't an option right now.

She'd best stay away from that church and everyone in it, especially Seth. He was a pastor, and even though she still loved the Lord, she had no desire to get caught up in the hypocritical life of church people who didn't practice what they preached.

Snatching up a newspaper from a table near a divan, she marched to the stairs. She'd read a while and try to get her mind off Seth. Then she'd hit the streets and check on some of the women she'd tried to befriend. If any of those holier-than-thou churchgoers happened to see her, so be it.

Her efforts were as much God's work as those of anyone who attended that place of worship. She didn't plan to shout her business from the rooftops, but she'd made up her mind. No more slipping around in the shadows, whatever the cost.

Chapter Three

Seth propped the shovel against a tree and leaned over the new headstone, thankful he had company. Typically he enjoyed caring for the grassy area behind the church, but this time he was happy Micah Jacobs had offered to help. Seth hadn't been out here for a couple of weeks but had noticed a few days ago that the area needed tending.

At least their church cemetery was sparsely occupied thus far. But the grass and weeds encroached into every nook and cranny, and the hot summer sun had taken its toll on the whitewash of the picket fence, already showing signs of peeling. Apparently the gentleman who had applied the paint hadn't been as thorough as he'd claimed.

Micah dusted his hands against the legs of his trousers. "I can help you again tomorrow if you'd like."

Seth felt tempted to accept the offer but finally shook his head. "You have enough of your own work. I have an idea, and since you're on the church board, I'd like to run it past you first."

"I'm all ears. You know I'm game for whatever you think is right." Micah leaned against the rough bark of the tree and smiled.

"I hope Mr. Beal and Mr. Thompson will feel the same. I was considering hiring a man to tend the graveyard and clean the church once or twice a week. The ladies have so much to do at their own homes, and I hate to ask for more."

"Do you have someone in mind?"

"A lot of Chinese are moving into the area and not all of them are employed. Maybe we could find a man who'd be interested in taking on a little extra work, as we can't offer full time."

Micah straightened and gave a slow nod. "I don't see any reason why not. It shouldn't cost much, and it would free up the ladies who do the cleaning. How about I stop by and chat with both of the gentlemen and get their opinion on the matter?"

Seth stuck out his hand. "Thank you, Micah. You've been a true friend, and I appreciate you."

Micah returned his grip. "Not as much as I do you. If it wasn't for you, I wouldn't have my business or my pride."

"God doesn't want us to stand on pride, my friend, but He does want us to feel good about the work He's given us to do. I can't lay claim to the success of your business—that is all due to your sound work ethic and God's blessing."

He clapped Micah on the back and grinned. "But I'm happy for any small part I played. Now I'd best go inside and retrieve my list then get to town and pick up a few supplies."

"I'll let you know as soon as I have the go-ahead from Beal and Thompson." Micah pivoted and struck out across the hard-packed dirt.

Seth stuffed his hands in his pockets and sauntered toward the one-story building with the attractive bell tower that he'd come to love over the past three years. His time at seminary had led him to believe the challenges of a pastorate might be overly taxing. While he'd encountered his share of trials, there had been nothing he hadn't been able to deal with.

For the most part the people in his congregation were kind and generous, and he'd not lacked for much since arriving. In fact, the biggest problems so far had been getting Mrs. Beal to agree to play a couple of new hymns on the organ, or encouraging Mrs. Evans to keep her own counsel.

His mind darted to Julia and a shadow slipped across his spirit, dampening his enthusiasm. As much as he hoped and prayed all was well in her life, something told him it wasn't—and the repercussions could affect him, as well.

Julia brushed her wayward brunette strands and then tucked her hair combs in a little tighter. She peered into the wavy mirror the hotel provided. While she'd never seen herself as particularly pretty, she'd always been grateful for her clear skin and average sized nose.

Her paternal grandmother had railed at the size of her own appendage during Julia's growing-up years. Grandmother had drummed it into her consciousness that she should be grateful for the petite nose inherited from her mother. Julia smiled at the memory.

Grandmother McKenzie was nothing if not blunt, but the older woman had shown her love in so many ways prior to her passing.

What she'd give for a cool bath or a dip in the Powder River. She'd seen children playing along the edges of the water, but she didn't think slipping off her shoes and stockings and raising her skirts to her knees to wade would meet with approval any more than some of her other activities. It would probably be best to forgo that temptation for the present.

She plucked a damp cloth off her bureau and swished it in the bowl of tepid water, then wrung it out and passed it over her face and neck. Oregon had always sounded like such a green, cool place with all the rivers, mountains and trees, that she'd had no idea early summer could be so hot.

Julia opened her door and stepped out into the close, hot hallway and gasped. At least there was a bit of a draft in her room, but no air moved in this musty, confined space. Rivulets of perspiration trickled between her shoulder blades, and she hurried down the steps. She didn't even glance toward the comfortable chairs in the lobby. Right now she wanted one thing—cool air.

She stepped out onto the boardwalk and paused, still not certain where she wanted to go. A gentle breeze wafted a tendril off her temple. *Heavenly.* Glancing down at her plain cotton skirt, she made a decision.

She would cool her feet and then go visit Mei and her family. She hadn't come West with visions of winning souls like some missionaries she knew, nor did she hope to win any contests for high esteem among the stalwart members of the community, but her passion burned to make a difference in the lives of downtrodden people. If she could make even one person's life easier, it was worth whatever sacrifice she was called to make.

Seth's pace slowed as he neared the river. Shouts of children mingled with the bark of a dog. Normally he'd speak to any parent sitting on the bank while their offspring played, but he shied from doing so today.

He had only another hour until the potluck and had hoped to find Julia resting at the hotel. But the walk to town had only brought disappointment when the hotel clerk informed him that Miss McKenzie had departed some time earlier.

He skirted a cluster of people, responding when one of them spoke, but he kept moving forward. Why hadn't Julia talked to him personally when she'd broken off their friendship? He'd assumed she'd gotten wind of his desire to be a pastor, and she'd hated the idea. But even then that hadn't made sense, since her father was a respected minister.

Seth strode toward the Powder River, walking around a large maple tree casting welcome shade in its path. He halted abruptly at the sight of a woman sitting on the bank, her bare feet and ankles exposed as she dangled them in the moving flow. She swiveled her head and gasped.

"Oh, pardon me. I didn't mean to intrude." All of a sudden he felt as though he might choke, as Julia's beautiful face stared up into his.

Julia froze, barely able to move as she met the gaze of the one man she longed—yet dreaded—to see. For seven years she'd regretted her hasty decision to break off their relationship so she could pursue her own desires—only to have that pursuit turn to dust and ashes. Her father had died not long after, and she'd been thrown to her own devices.

Thankfully, he'd left her a small inheritance and her mother's jewelry, but she wasn't allowed to stay in the only home she'd ever known. The people of his large, affluent church were in a hurry to find a replacement, with little thought to his only surviving family member.

Abruptly, her life had changed, and not for the better. She'd considered finding Seth and begging his forgiveness, but she was certain she'd damaged his pride to the point he'd turn his back on her like everyone else. A good thing she hadn't.

The thought of submitting herself to a critical congregation again stuck in her craw. It had taken three years of scrubbing dirty dishes in a restaurant before she'd struck out on her own, then three more years working at a hospital as a nurse's helper before heading west. She could have stayed in Omaha, but she'd heard stories of the West and dreamed of the chance to help people in need.

Jerking her skirt down over her ankles, Julia struggled to regain her composure and push the memories where they belonged—into the dim recesses of the past. It was too late to undo the wrong she'd done when she'd sent that letter. Almost without a thought, she'd thrown away the only man she'd ever cared for.

"Seth? What are you doing here? Don't you have a church function starting soon?"

Seth ran his palm over his chin. Questions that she couldn't quite decipher flitted across his handsome countenance, chased by something almost like longing—but that must surely be her imagination creating whimsies, due to her earlier thoughts.

He nodded. "I needed a walk to clear my thoughts. I'll leave you alone, as I'm sure I've intruded enough for one day. I do hope you'll forgive me."

"Nonsense. There's nothing to forgive. It's nice to see you again." Julia scrambled to her feet and straightened her skirt, then realized her high-topped shoes and stockings were still on the grass. A warm flush crept up her cheeks. What must Seth think? "Um—would you please excuse me for a moment so I can slip my shoes on?"

His cheeks blazed into brilliant color, and he turned away. "Certainly. But I can as easily return home. Unless you'd care for an escort to your hotel?" Seth rocked on his heels as Julia sat back down and quickly donned her stockings and shoes.

"I'm finished now, thank you." Julia waited until he'd turned, noting the warm glow still suffusing his face. "It's not necessary that you go out of your way to walk me home. Besides, you'll barely have time to reach the church before the social starts."

"About that." Seth stepped closer and extended his hand. "Please let me help you up."

She hesitated a moment and then slipped her fingers into his, and a decided thrill smote her as she did so. "Thank you." His strength surprised her as he lifted her easily from her position on the grass.

Julia relaxed her hold, but Seth continued to clutch her hand, gazing down into her upturned face. Everything within her rioted as she gazed into his eyes. Her heart skipped a beat and plunged ahead like a horse off the starting line.

Seth drew her an inch or two closer, and his grip tightened. "Julia." He barely breathed the word through slightly parted lips. "I didn't realize how much I'd missed you—until now." His eyes darkened, and he touched a strand of hair that had loosened and curled against her cheek.

His fingers grazed her cheek, leaving a tingling sensation. More than anything Julia longed to lean into his caress and raise her lips. This man's quiet strength and compassionate nature had always called to her, even when she'd run from him, wanting to experience life before she settled down. How foolish she'd been to think anything else could be more satisfying than spending her life with Seth.

A child shrieked in the distance and Julia shivered, suddenly waking up to where they were and how this might appear. She'd already sullied her reputation with some of the women in his church by visiting questionable areas of town, and she didn't care to destroy his calling or ministry, no matter how she longed to have him draw her into his arms.

She took a step back and forced a smile. She wasn't the right woman for him, and the sooner he realized it, the better for them both. "I'm sorry, Seth, but the past is behind us, and we should move on."

He jerked as though burned with the business end of a branding iron. Another warm flush rose in his cheeks, but he didn't remove his gaze.

"Be that as it may, I would be very pleased if you'd consider attending the social. Katherine Jacobs and her family will be there, and I know they'd love to get better acquainted." He extended his arm. "Please, let me at least accompany you. And there are several other ladies whose company I believe you'd enjoy."

She slipped her hand under his arm and shrugged. "I think not. I'm not prepared and have nothing to bring."

Seth pressed her hand to his side for such a short space of time that Julia wasn't sure if she'd imagined it, then he swung down the path across the sparsely wooded area toward the road and the bridge, drawing her with him.

"The women of our church bring so much food we always have leftovers. Why not stop for a few minutes at least?"

Temptation to spend even a few more minutes in Seth's company warred with common sense. "I'm afraid I won't fit in. You saw how Mrs. Evans treated me this morning. I don't care to endure that type of thing whenever I set foot inside a church, but it's bound to happen. At least, for as long as I continue in my pursuits."

Seth glanced at her, his expression concerned. "Since you bring it up, may I ask what those pursuits entail? Are you in some kind of trouble, Julia? Is there any way I can help?"

"In trouble?" Julia jerked to a stop and withdrew her hand. "Whatever are you implying? Do you think I was working at the saloon?"

His brows drew down in apparent puzzlement, and he stood without moving. "No, I'm not implying anything of the sort. The Julia McKenzie I remember would never have taken a job in such a place. I'm quite confident there's an entirely different reason for your presence in that area. I was simply offering to help if there's something that concerns or worries you."

Julia continued to look at him intently, and her thudding heart calmed at the truth she read there. He wasn't censoring her or accusing her of poor behavior. He cared.

She resumed her hold on the crook of his arm. "Thank you, Seth. I appreciate that more than you know. But I'm not sure how much to share."

His step faltered, then he squeezed her hand once again. "Tell me only what you wish. I'd like to be your friend again, if that's possible."

He focused straight ahead. "I know we parted on rather unusual terms, but it hasn't changed my regard for you. As a friend, of course." His words were cloaked in discouragement. "Nothing more—unless you tell me you desire it."

Julia's heart jolted as guilt over the thought of hurting him smote her. She still wasn't completely certain how she felt about Seth. Seven years was a long time, and from what she could tell, he'd changed as much or more than she.

They'd been compatible at one time, but would the passage of time and altered circumstances have transformed them to the point where a relationship wouldn't be possible?

The direction her life had taken would only get him in trouble with his congregation, no matter how much she might like to return to their previous relationship. "Friends. Naturally. I'd like that, Seth. Thank you."

His face fell and his lips firmed, then he stretched them into what passed as a weak smile. "As you wish."

She bit her lip, not willing to reveal more. Not yet. Not now. "And I'll accompany you to the social, if you believe I'm appropriately dressed."

His glance flitted to her face and then dropped. "You're lovely no matter what you wear, and your clothing is perfectly appropriate."

"Thank you. Now may I ask you a question?"

He raised his brows. "Of course. Anything."

"You hardly seem like the same man I knew in Omaha. You were always kind, but you had a wild streak. Papa worried about that when we started seeing one another."

She hesitated, wondering if she should continue, but she must know the truth. "He feared you would do something foolish or run off, if you tired of marriage."

The muscles of his arm clenched, then he drew in a deep breath and released it in a slow whoosh. "I can see why he'd think that. After I left the orphanage, I had no moral compass. Most of my life growing up, I believed people only acted like they cared because they wanted something. When I met you, I realized that wasn't always the case. I had a new purpose, and attending your father's church gave me hope. He was a true man of God and lived what he preached.

"I'd never seen that before—in fact, I made a firm commitment to the Lord the day before receiving your letter, and I felt a strong call to follow in your father's footsteps."

He glanced at her, his face solemn. "I planned to tell you the next night, but I never got the chance."

Guilt wove its way through Julia's body, and she shivered. "I'm so sorry. I wish I'd known."

Seth hunched a shoulder. "It was all so new. I had to deal with bitterness and anger when I got your letter. Then pride set in and wouldn't allow me to seek you out.

"I quit attending church for a year, and when God finally got through to my stubborn heart, I chose a different place of worship, worried I might see you or your father. It wasn't long after that I left for seminary. When I finished, I came to Baker City and took my first pastorate."

Julia wanted to retreat and run to her room. Seth had battled bitterness and anger. Of course he would have— why should she have thought otherwise? And it was her fault. He'd seen her as a Christian—someone he could trust—someone whose life gave him new purpose, and she'd thrown that away with one thoughtless letter.

Even if she hadn't been ready to marry, she should have done things differently. Yes, she was young, but that was no excuse. If only she could go back and do it over again. "I had no idea. You've been so kind since you met me again—I'd think you wouldn't want to speak to me."

Seth patted her hand still slipped inside the crook of his arm. "Nonsense. I forgave you long ago, Julia. Let's not talk of it anymore. We're almost to the church."

They continued the rest of the way in silence, but the walk passed in agony. Julia had too much to think about—her rejection of Seth must have accentuated how alone he was in the world.

Now that she'd lost both her parents, she understood so much more than she did as a young woman.

He said he'd forgiven, but how could a man truly forgive the slight to his pride, as well as the deep hurt she'd unwittingly inflicted? It would be better to go to her room and never darken the doors of Seth's church—or life—again.

And no doubt Mrs. Evans would be in attendance at the social this evening. If the woman said one more unkind word to Seth or herself, she'd leave, to save Seth more humiliation. Julia didn't care to jeopardize her work among the downtrodden of this town by spreading out her business before the judgment of women like Mrs. Evans and her ilk.

She'd seen that behavior too many times in the Omaha hospital that served the rich and poor alike, not to mention the hoity-toity women of her father's congregation after he'd died.

Suddenly, she'd become a liability—someone who lived in a house the elders wanted for a new family—and she was hurting too much to accept help from the few who offered compassion.

As they neared the building, Julia loosened her grip from Seth's arm. His brows rose, but he didn't speak. He must know it wouldn't be socially acceptable for the pastor of a church to be seen escorting a single woman to a social function, unless he made it clear they were courting. Not unless he wanted more tongues to wag than already were.

Seth nodded to a family mounting the steps and swung wide the door, allowing Julia and the group of six to enter ahead of him. Suddenly, Julia felt alone as every eye in the entryway turned her way, including that of Mrs. Evans.

Julia straightened and smiled, determined to endure this for Seth. His kindness toward her would not go unrewarded.

The door opened again, and Katherine Jacobs entered ahead of a man who must be her husband, along with their three children and her mother.

Katherine's face lit as she noticed Julia. "Miss McKenzie. How delightful to see you here. I hope you'll consider sitting with us, as I'd love to get better acquainted."

Relief coursed through Julia, and she relaxed. "I'd enjoy that, thank you."

Suddenly, the door slammed open, nearly bouncing off the wall behind it. Lee Meng stood revealed, twisting his round black cap in his hands until Julia thought he'd rend it in two.

"Missy Ju-la, Missy Ju-la! Mei say come to house quick! She need help now!"

The last thing Julia saw as she sprang for the door was Mrs. Evans, mouth agape, but Julia barely noticed. She grasped Meng's fingers and ran, not caring one whit what that old gossip-monger thought. Her duty lay with this little boy and whatever had befallen his sister, come what may from the people in Seth's congregation.

Chapter Four

Seth grabbed his hat off a peg and bolted across the foyer, intent on helping if he could. The boy's broken English was poor, but it sounded like someone he cared about was in serious trouble. He made it as far as the front door when Mrs. Evans' bulky frame blocked his way.

She stood with arms crossed over her chest, a glare marring her features. "Where do you think you're going, Pastor?"

Seth halted so fast he thought he'd plow right over the top of the woman, and at the moment he wasn't sure he'd even stop to pick her up if she hit the floor. "Where I'm needed. To a family in crisis."

"Humph. Your duty is with this church and the people you serve, not some Chinese boy who barely speaks our language."

She stabbed her finger at his chest. "Keep in mind that we pay your salary. You are first and foremost obligated to us."

"My duty, Mrs. Evans, is to God first, and any person who is in need, next, whether they be a member of this church or someone from a foreign country. It does not matter to God what a man's skin color is, and it doesn't to me, either. Now please, step aside and let me pass."

Her face contorted even more, if that were possible, but she didn't budge. "No, sir. I shall not. And if you go out that door I'll ask that a meeting of the church elders be convened."

Micah Jacobs stepped forward. "There's no call to be upset. If Pastor Seth feels there's a need to minister to a person in the community, we should let him go with our blessing."

Wilma Roberts and Frances Cooper moved up on either side of the pair and Mrs. Roberts took Mrs. Evans by the arm. "Come now, dear, let the pastor pass, or he'll never catch up with Miss McKenzie."

She tugged at the woman's arm, and Mrs. Evans reluctantly moved aside. "There's no reason to call the elders, as at least two of them are here tonight and saw what happened. It's certainly a man of God's responsibility to help those in need."

Seth jumped for the door and took the outer steps two at a time, thankful it was still daylight and there would be little foot or wagon traffic this late on a Sunday afternoon.

Obviously Julia and the boy headed to Chinatown. Now to catch up with them before they entered the child's home and he lost sight of them altogether.

He kept on through the streets at a steady pace, barely under a hard run, praying all the while that God would give him guidance and help. He'd had to deal with more than one tragedy since coming to this town, including the death of Katherine's first husband shortly after he'd arrived.

He shuddered, remembering that mining accident all too well, and praying the same thing hadn't befallen someone in the boy's family. He'd said something about Lee Mei, a woman or girl's name.

"Oh, Lord, be with them all, whatever is wrong." He huffed the words through parted lips, his breath short as he continued his quick pace.

Rounding the final corner that brought him within sight of Chinatown, he slowed to a fast walk, peering ahead at the dark-clad people lining the street. A flash of blue appeared beyond a cluster of men standing outside a tiny home, and Julia disappeared with the boy through the door of what looked like little more than a shack.

"Thank you, Lord." Now all he had to do was pray the men guarding the door would allow him to enter. The last thing he wanted was for Julia and the boy to be trapped in a dangerous situation.

For that matter, from the scowls on the men's faces and the dark mutters, he wasn't certain how safe he'd be. His heart caught in his throat as he pushed through the crowd.

A light breeze sprang up and the door of the shack swayed open a few inches, and the men were too busy talking to pay him any mind. Lowering his head, he pushed past the last cluster and reached the door. Too bad he couldn't understand what they were saying, but hopefully, he'd know the extent of the problem soon.

Julia knelt beside the prone figure on the bed, relieved that it wasn't Mei. She stared at the young woman standing on the far side. "Your father?"

The girl nodded, her face stricken. "Yes, my papa. Mei afraid to ask doctor to come. I no have money to pay. Doctor not like come to Chinese house, so Mei send Meng to get Miss Julia. You fix him?" Dark pools of pain reflected from the depths of her eyes as she turned the full force of them on Julia.

Julia touched the base of the man's throat, feeling for a pulse. "I don't know how much I can do, Mei. I've only had basic nursing training, and I have no medicine or bandages with me, but I'll try. What happened?"

She shuddered at the torn, bloody shirt and peeled back the heavy layers of cloth, revealing an ugly gash at the top of his chest. At least the bleeding had stopped.

It didn't seem life-threatening, but she had no idea how much blood he'd lost. "We need to get this clean. Do you have hot water and clean rags?"

Mei nodded and motioned to one of her countrymen hovering inside the door. "Bring water from pot outside, and cloths. Hurry."

Julia peered over her shoulder, hoping the man would follow directions quickly, and she gave a start. Seth Russell stood on the inside of the canvas that hung over the opening.

Relief coursed through her, leaving little room to wonder why he was here or how long ago he'd entered. Right now all that mattered was that someone was here who might help. "Seth, please come here."

He hurried forward and sank to his knees beside the rough pallet that served as a bed. "What can I do?"

Julia prayed she'd see something in the room that could cleanse the wound besides water. Mei kept the tight space clean, but every personal belonging in the shack shouted the poverty of these people.

"I wish I knew. I'll do the best I can cleaning the wound, but he desperately needs a doctor."

"Then I'll go get one." Seth started to push to his feet.

Julia touched his wrist. "I'm not sure he'll come. From what I've seen, there's a lot of prejudice against these people. Most white men don't want to enter Chinatown unless it's life or death."

Seth stared at the man on the pallet. "I'd say this qualifies. Not for the doctor, but surely for this man. Will you be all right while I'm gone? Is it safe? The men outside appeared angry. If this man dies, will you become a target for that anger?"

"I don't know, but right now it's not important. Someone must stay here and care for him. I think I'm safer here than making my way back through the crowd and to the doctor's office. It would be dusk by the time I can get there and return."

She squeezed his hand and then released it. "Thank you for offering, Seth."

He gave her a long look as if hesitant about leaving, but finally nodded and rose. "Certainly." His eyes swept the interior. "Meng, will you stay with the lady and take care of her?"

The boy jerked upright from where he'd been slumped, and a grin covered his face. "Yes, Mister. Meng take charge. He do a good job caring for Missy Ju-la, you see."

"Good boy." Seth touched the child's arm for a brief moment. "I'll hurry." Without another word, he pivoted and disappeared through the canvas barrier, leaving Julia feeling as empty and alone as an orphaned child on Christmas day.

Seth clenched his fist, emotions warring inside that he'd worked hard to suppress all these years. He wanted to hit something, but it wouldn't do any good, even if his standing as a pastor would have allowed it. He'd been to two doctors so far and been turned away by both.

The first man was in surgery and couldn't leave, and the second seemed more concerned with remaining available to his 'Christian' patients who might wander in, than attending a severely injured man in Chinatown.

Why hadn't he realized the depth of prejudice against these people since arriving in Oregon? Had it taken Julia's involvement to open his eyes? If so, it was deplorable that he hadn't noticed on his own.

He hadn't had occasion to deal with the residents of Chinatown in the past, but neither had he reached out to that segment of the local population, something he'd remedy in the future. Right now he must find someone to help patch that man up and get back to Julia as quickly as possible.

He stepped up on the boardwalk in front of a tiny building with a doctor sign hanging on a post and rapped on the door.

"Enter. It's not locked." A gruff voice emanated through the thin walls.

Seth eased open the door. A stooped, gray-haired man wearing a suit with frayed cuffs and a white shirt that had seen better days looked up from his desk. He adjusted his spectacles and peered through the dense lenses. "Can I help you, son?"

If he hadn't already tried every doctor in town, Seth would have turned around and headed out of there. "Yes, sir, I hope so. I left a friend tending an injured man who has a deep gash. The wound needs cleaning and more than likely stitches. Can you come?"

"Certainly. I'll get my bag and add some carbolic soap and salve. That might help stave off infection. Wait just a moment." He disappeared behind a curtain that led into another room, then returned in matter of minutes. "I'm ready. Do we need my buggy, or is it walking distance?"

Seth hesitated, not willing to lie to the man but hating to be spurned once again. He sucked in a sharp breath and expelled it. "It's only a few blocks."

He jerked his head. "Over in Chinatown." He stood frozen in the middle of the room, waiting for the expected response.

The doctor didn't hesitate but headed toward the door. "Then let's get going. No time to stand around lollygagging, young man. Hop to it."

He disappeared through the door, and Seth jumped to follow, joy permeating his entire body.

Seth kept pace with the doctor, amazed at the older man's long stride and even breathing. At this rate they'd get back to the shack faster than he'd expected. Hopefully the injured man hadn't bled too much to save. He shot up a prayer, and added another one for Julia.

He hadn't spoken lightly when he'd asked about her safety. It was all well and good for a man of the cloth to make benevolent visits during day-time hours, but a young, single woman had no business going to that part of town unattended, and he planned to tell Julia so as soon as this crisis passed.

Julia pressed another clean cloth against the wound, praying Seth would hurry. The men outside the door were growing more agitated with each passing minute. It was doubtful they'd harm her, but without a clear understanding of what had happened to cause the injury to Mei's father, she couldn't be certain. "Mei?"

The girl lifted her bowed head, but not before Julia saw her lips moving in what appeared to be silent prayer. "Yes, Miss Julia?" She clutched a post nearby and started to pull herself to her feet. "What you need? I get it."

"No, nothing. Please. Sit." Julia waited until the younger woman sank back beside the pallet. "Can you tell me what happened to your father? Was he injured at the mine?"

Mei's dark gaze dropped. "Not at the mine."

Dread plucked at Julia's heart. "Where then?"

"Saloon. Man there cut him with big knife."

Julia gaped. Things like this happened from time to time, but this was the first instance she'd seen. "What was he doing at the saloon?" She had a very good idea, but it wouldn't be fair to Mei to assume the worst. "He wasn't there to drink, was he?"

"No." Mei's voice held harsh insistence. "Chinaman not allowed to drink with white men. He there for me." A whimper escaped her throat.

"Tell me, Mei. I want to help if I can." Julia reached across the unconscious man and touched the girl's cheek. "Please?"

"Poppa come home after he gone long, long time. Meng tell him I at work. He come to find me—let me know he safe. He come in through back door and ask for me. Tell the man he my poppa and need to talk to me. Man say no. Go away. No belong there."

She gripped her hands together in front of her chest. "Poppa say only a minute he stay. Not bother, but to talk. I hear them speak loud from the other room and I run fast, happy Poppa is home safe. Man shove Poppa against wall and hits him. Says he no belong there. Get out." Her breaths were coming in short gasps now.

Julia wished she could draw the girl into a hug, but she knew that the best thing for Mei right now was to tell the story and get it behind her. "What happened next?"

"I scream. Tell him to not hurt Poppa, he mean no harm. He happy to see me. Man hits me. Hard." She raised her fingers to her cheek and winced, and only then did Julia notice the welt on her cheekbone.

"Make Poppa mad. He never hurt anyone. Never argue with white man. But he not like to see me get hit. He try to step between me and man. Not to fight with him, only to protect me."

Julia nodded. "The man pulled a knife? He cut your father?"

"Yes. Stab him and push him out the door. He grab my arm and say "Get to work", but I shove him hard. He stumble and fall and hit his head on the wall. Poppa's friend from the mine wait at end of alley and help us get home. He bring other men and tell what happen. They want to go to saloon and find man who did this, but I say no. My boss, he kill them all. Boss not care about Chinamen. He think they not people."

Julia knew it was true, but she hated hearing such awful things spoken out loud. But what good did it do to keep quiet about this kind of hatred and prejudice? People would never change if they weren't confronted with their bigotry and injustice. But Mei was right. It would only get more people injured or killed if they tried to avenge her father.

It was one thing to grumble about the man who'd done this, but quite another for these usually placid men to follow through with their threats. "You were wise to tell them no, Mei. I wish it weren't true, but you're probably right. If they went to the saloon, more men would be hurt and possibly die."

The curtain on the front door was pushed back, allowing in much-needed light from extra lanterns hanging outside. Seth held it aside and waited for an older, stoop-shouldered man to enter, then Seth followed, letting the canvas fall into place.

Julia glanced at him. "Are the men outside still upset? Do you think it would be wise to leave the door open to allow more light in?"

Seth hesitated. "Miss Lee might be better able to make that decision."

Mei looked from one to the other. "My poppa's friends not hurt anyone here." She motioned to a silent man waiting inside the door. "Leave door open, and bring in more lanterns."

The older man who'd accompanied Seth dropped to his knees beside Julia and lifted the rag covering the wound. "What happened?"

Julia gestured at the injured man. "This is Mr. Lee. He was stabbed by someone at the saloon while trying to protect his daughter."

He gave a curt nod, taking in the dim shack. "I'll need one person to help me and better light. Have any of you any nursing experience?"

Seth stepped forward. "I can help."

Julia shook her head. "I spent nearly three years at a hospital volunteering, doctor. I'd like to stay, if you'll have me."

"Fine. Both of you then. But I'll need the rest of the people in the room to leave. It's too crowded and hard to move. Can you tell them to go outside?" He didn't wait for a reply but opened his bag and rummaged inside.

Julia reached across to Mei and lightly touched her arm. "Would you take your brother outside? I don't want to disturb your grandmother or offend her, but would you ask if she's willing to go as well?"

She gestured at the older woman still sitting in a nearby corner, rocking gently back and forth. "I know you want to stay and help, but it might be best if you care for her out by the fire and give the doctor more room to work. I promise I'll let you know if you're needed."

Seth stepped aside as the doctor exited the shack with Julia on his heels, worry niggling at his mind. "Do you think he'll recover?" The murmuring of the men outside had ceased, but an uneasy atmosphere still prevailed among the dozen or so still standing nearby.

The older man wiped his forehead with a slightly ragged handkerchief then tucked it back into his pocket. "He will. There was some blood loss, but Miss Lee got it stopped in time. I was able to treat the wound with carbolic acid and stitch it closed. I'll stop by tomorrow to change the dressing and apply more salve. As long as we avoid infection, he should make a nice recovery."

Julia touched the doctor's sleeve. "I'll see that you get paid. I can't tell you how much we appreciate that you were willing to come. I'm sure not anyone else would have."

He shrugged. "No need for payment, young lady. I'll bring some of my laundry by and that should make us square. As for the other 'gentlemen' of my profession, I have nothing to say in that regard, other than they should reconsider the oath they took upon completing their training."

Seth grinned and extended his hand, gripping the doctor's in a warm handshake. "Thank you, sir. May I walk you back to your office? I'll be escorting Miss McKenzie, as well, but I'm sure she won't mind walking you home."

"No thank you. I have another patient to check on. I'll be fine." He settled his hat and buttoned his jacket. "Have a good evening." Pivoting, he strode through the cluster of men.

Seth watched the man leave then turned to Julia. "Is there anything else you need to do here?"

He nodded at the silent group huddled around the open fire in the barren yard. "It's not wise for you to walk home alone. I'd like to escort you, if I may."

She hesitated and then accepted his proffered arm. "Thank you. That might be sensible. I've already said goodbye to Mei and Meng, so we can leave now." Falling into step beside him, she kept her gaze straight ahead as they passed the silent knot of men.

They walked in silence until they were out of sight of the last of the shanty town. Seth peeked at Julia's calm profile, wondering if now would be a good time to discuss his concerns. Probably better to broach the subject now since there was no guarantee when he'd get to talk to her again privately.

The church wasn't an option, and it wasn't like he could call on her in her room at the hotel. If only she lived somewhere else—of course, he could ask her out to dinner if she'd come, but he wasn't so sure she'd accept a formal request. An idea flitted through his mind, and he smiled. He'd follow up on that as soon as he could speak to Katherine or Micah.

A handful of lanterns were hung on pegs outside the doors of businesses along the main street of town, making it easier to see in the evening gloom. Seth slowed his pace as they stopped at the edge of the side road that emptied onto the street.

No sense in rushing out and getting trampled by a horse or wagon. The town had grown busy enough to still have a light spattering of traffic in the evenings. He squeezed Julia's arm, hoping to bring her out of her reverie. "Julia?"

"Hmm?" She turned to face him, her brows drawn together in a slight pucker. "I'm sorry, were you speaking to me?"

"I'd like to ask something, if you'll be kind enough to listen."

"Certainly. I could do no less after the help you've given. Should we keep walking or stop for a moment?"

Seth looked both directions. "Let's get across the road and over to the boardwalk and sit on one of the benches, if you don't mind. We'll be close to your hotel. I suppose we could talk in the foyer since the restaurant is closed. But I don't know how busy the hotel might be at this time of night, and I'd appreciate a bit of privacy."

"All right." She tucked her hand deeper into the crook of his elbow as he strode quickly across the dirt expanse.

His pulse beat rapidly as her fingers tightened before he helped her onto the boardwalk. When she settled onto a bench in front of Snider's General Store, a sense of loss assailed him.

Shaking it off, he sank down beside her, leaving an acceptable distance between them, lest anyone notice. The last thing Julia needed was for more tongues to wag. "What you did for the Lee family was extraordinary."

Her face lit with a deep-seated joy. "Thank you."

Seth almost changed his mind about what he'd planned to say. Almost, but not quite. This was not only important for her reputation, but for her safety as well. "I hope you'll hear me out."

She shifted and angled her body toward him. "You sound quite serious for someone who felt what I did was extraordinary."

"I'm afraid so. I know I have no right to offer advice, but for the sake of our past friendship, I pray you'll take me seriously."

Julia dipped her head, but her smile vanished. "Go on." She smoothed the folds of her skirt.

In for a penny, in for a pound. He'd started this and must press on. "I don't think you should go to Chinatown again."

Her hands stilled. "That's absurd. Certainly I'll go. I promised Mei I'd check on her father tomorrow. Also, she plans to return to work at the saloon, and I said I'd accompany her. If she doesn't have someone with her, she's apt to be beaten when she returns for running out before her shift ended tonight."

She lifted her chin. "I'll not allow that to happen."

Seth straightened his spine and strengthened his resolve. He'd forgotten how determined Julia could be when she set her mind on accomplishing something.

"I can easily swing by and check on the family, as well as walk Miss Lee to work. Remember the doctor plans to come tomorrow, as well. There's really no need for you to put yourself at risk."

Her eyes narrowed. "Pray tell, exactly how am I putting myself at risk?" The words were calm, deliberate, but coated with iron.

"Your presence in Chinatown does that, as well as being in or near the saloon. There are dangerous men in this town, and if you didn't notice, a number of the Lee family's friends were quite unhappy at the treatment he received."

"That's utter nonsense. They would never harm me. Mei has told them I'm helping her."

"Be that as it may, you're a single white woman going into Chinatown alone, not to mention accompanying Miss Lee to the saloon or going in to check on her from time to time. It's not safe, and you need to stop. I assume that's what you were doing the first day I met you in the alley?"

She hunched a shoulder. "What if it was?" Her tone had gone from calm to border-line belligerent. "I'm a grown woman who makes her own decisions. I will not have anyone telling me what to do or where I can go."

Seth bit back a groan and worked to suppress the frustration building inside. He wasn't handling this well at all. "I'm aware of that, Julia. But you have no father or husband here to watch out for your welfare. We used to be friends at one time, and had things not gone as they did, we might have become more."

He waited, not wanting to bring up yet another delicate subject, but praying she'd give him a glimpse into the reason why she'd run away, leaving nothing more than a perfunctory letter that told him next to nothing.

She pressed her lips together. "I'm not in need of a protector, thank you very much. And I think you overestimate the danger. This is a civilized town. No man is going to hurt a white woman."

"A man stabbed Mr. Lee, and from the appearance of her face, Miss Lee is at risk for rough handling, as well.

So yes, I do believe there is significant danger, and not only to the Chinese."

Julia's chin tilted ever so slightly higher. "I agree. There is danger to the Chinese, which is deplorable, but not to a decent white woman with a good reputation."

"I've lived here for several years, and I disagree. If you were in the company of a man, or even of another woman, you'd be safe. In fact, if you simply stay out of Chinatown and the back alleys and travel the well-trodden public streets, you'll be fine.

"But for your own safety I must insist you don't venture to Chinatown any more—at least unaccompanied—and never to the alleys behind the saloons. If you have a need to see Miss Lee or her family, let me know, and I'll take you. Will you at least do that much?"

Julia worked to keep a firm grip on her temper, but she wanted to jump from the bench and fly away from this place—and this man. Insist that she follow his orders? Not likely. He might have been something to her once—she might even regret the decision she'd made back then—but that gave him no right to tell her what to do now.

"I'm sorry, but I won't make any promises. Mei's people need me, and I see it as my mission to help them. No one else seems to care, so I'm not going to stay away. I'd think the pastors in town would rally to their aid, but as they haven't, I will."

She pushed to her feet. "I'm close to my hotel, and I can see myself the rest of the way. Please don't bother yourself further with my needs."

"Julia, wait. Please. I don't think you understand. I'm concerned with the plight of the Chinese, but that's a large issue that will take time and effort to correct. Right now I'm more concerned with your safety, not to mention your reputation." Seth stood as well.

Julia steeled herself against Seth's bereft expression and took a step away. "I understand well enough, *Pastor* Russell, and I don't agree with you. I can take care of myself."

Maybe he hadn't meant to be bossy, but he'd still stepped in where he had no right.

Besides, she didn't for an instant believe she could be in danger. Mei's people knew she was there to help, and no man would touch a white woman on the streets. She pivoted and walked away, praying Seth didn't find it necessary to follow.

No footsteps clunked on the boardwalk behind her, but instead of the relief she expected, regret flooded her, leaving her legs weak. Had she chased away the only man who'd truly cared?

She straightened her spine and refused to look back. It had been a long, hard fight to earn a place of independence. If her father hadn't left her mother's jewelry as a small inheritance, her life surely would have been different. As it was, the money from selling most of the pieces was nearly gone—at best, only a couple months room and board remained.

Maybe she should ask the doctor if he needed an assistant or apply for work at some of the places in town.

But she'd come to Baker City with a purpose—to help the downtrodden women of Chinatown to better their lives. Could she watch out for them and work at the same time? On the other hand, could she keep helping them if she didn't replenish her funds soon?

It was all too much. Julia yanked open the door of the Arlington Hotel and slipped inside, wondering again at her wayward heart that urged her to run back to Seth and throw herself into his arms.

Shaking off the thought, she crossed the foyer. For all she knew the man was in love with another woman by now, although she'd seen no evidence of a fiancée at the church.

A warm glow suffused her cheeks. And he certainly hadn't acted as though he had feelings for another woman while holding her in his arms by the river. But that didn't mean he still cared deeply about her.

His concern for her safety could simply be that of an old friend, watching out for a woman he'd once been interested in because it was the right thing to do. Nothing more.

She pushed away the memory of the time at the river. She'd interpreted more into his action than he'd intended, she was sure of it. He'd only said he'd missed her. Friends missed one another after a long time apart, didn't they?

Maybe she'd only imagined the gleam in his eyes as he'd leaned toward her. She bit back a groan. Why hadn't she waited and not pushed him away? She knew why—she'd been angry that he'd tried to tell her what to do—that he didn't trust her judgment about where she went or whom she chose to help.

She fumbled in her reticule for her key and then plunged it into the lock. Right now all she wanted to do was fall into bed and forget everything—her father, this town, her own needs—everything, that was, except the man who aggravated her to no end, but who still called to her heart.

Chapter Five

Late the next morning, Julia coiled her hair into a knot at the nape of her neck and peered into the mirror. She looked like she felt—a woman with puffy eyes and pale skin who'd barely slept more than an hour or two. What she wouldn't give right now to sink into a tub of hot water, but she couldn't squander her money on such luxuries.

A tap at her door spun her around, her heart thudding. She wasn't expecting a visitor. It certainly wouldn't be appropriate for Seth to come to her room. Julia sucked in a long breath, then released it slowly and walked to the door. She opened it a crack and peeked out.

A desk clerk stood with his hands clasped behind his back, rocking on his heels, but he came to attention as she widened the gap. "Hello, Miss McKenzie. A lady asked me to deliver this to you." He thrust out an envelope.

"Thank you." She waited until he'd swiveled and disappeared down the hall before breaking the seal and removing the note. She quickly took in the beautiful script, allowing her gaze to go to the last line.

Katherine Jacobs.

Julia smiled and relaxed. Taking her time, she perused the note again. A luncheon invitation with Mrs. Jacobs, her mother, Mrs. Cooper, and two others whom Julia had little acquaintance with as of yet, Mrs. Wilma Roberts and her niece Beth. From what she remembered of her visit to church, these women had been kind and courteous, not once expressing disapproval.

Should she have sent a note back with the clerk? Reading it through again, Julia heaved a sigh of relief. The ladies planned to take luncheon in the dining room here at the hotel in thirty minutes and hoped she'd join them. Perfect. It had been too long since she'd had time with other congenial women.

After she slipped out of her everyday dress, she set it aside and opened her trunk. She withdrew a soft blue satin with a fitted waist and rounded neckline, the sleeves shorter than she was used to, but all the rage back east. Simple, yet elegant.

The color enhanced her eyes and showed up the tint of auburn in her otherwise brown hair. This was the type of dress she'd wear to evening affairs at home in bygone years. The gown made her feel special, and after the past few days, she needed to experience that emotion again.

She smoothed the lace at her throat and smiled at her reflection. If Papa could see her now, how proud he'd be. Her heart lurched as another face made his appearance in her mind's eye.

What would Seth think? Would she see admiration, or would he only view her as a friend? Even after the things he'd said, trying to tell her what she could and couldn't do, she still valued his opinion. Maybe even more than that, she longed for his appreciation.

Wandering to her bureau, she reached for the top drawer then hesitated. She hadn't opened that cedar box in years, so why stir those memories now? She took a step back and considered. It was foolish to place so much emphasis on something so old that probably had crumbled to dust by now.

Hands shaking, she slid open the drawer and withdrew a small, hand-crafted cedar box. The hinges moved smoothly as she lifted the top and breathed deeply of the aromatic fragrance.

A bit of tissue was tucked in the corner, and Julia carefully removed the paper and peered underneath. Her breath caught and stilled. The dried Forget-Me-Not flowers were almost as blue as the day Seth presented them on her front porch. She'd pressed them between the pages of a book, then tucked them away in this box.

Tears pooled as recollections of their sweet times together flooded her mind. All these years—she'd known they were here—but she hadn't thrown them away, either. Had the fact that she'd heard a rumor about Seth moving to Baker City figured more into her decision to come here than she'd been willing to admit?

She brushed the moisture away and choked back a sob, then bit her lip hard. Enough of these thoughts. After flipping the paper back over the flowers, Julia closed the lid and shoved the box into the drawer where it belonged. She couldn't give in to the past. Her real reason for coming to this town hadn't changed, no matter how many regrets she might have.

Sinking into a chair in the corner of the room, she stared out the window, thankful for the half hour to rest and compose herself before the ladies arrived. Julia leaned against the high, upholstered wing-back chair, and then fixed her mind on Mei and her family. If only she could find a means to change their circumstances in a way that would matter.

The minutes ticked by, and suddenly Julia jerked upright and looked at the clock on her bureau. She sprang to her feet, in danger of being late for her luncheon.

Stepping to the mirror, she studied herself one last time. A rebellious curl had sprung out of hiding again. There was no help for it. She gently worked a matching strand from the other side and allowed the two short curls to dangle on each side of her face. Not too bad, and it would have to do.

She scurried to the door and then down the hallway, thankful she'd been given a room on the ground floor and needn't attempt the stairs in heeled, lace-up boots. She was used to much lower heels, but this gown warranted something a bit more special.

Julia slowed her pace as she crossed the carpeted foyer and then stopped at the door of the dining room, sweeping the area before her. Her heart sank when she didn't see the ladies. Had they changed their minds and decided to go elsewhere? She pivoted to return to her room, embarrassed that she'd wasted so much time primping.

"Pardon me." Seth's voice roused her, barely in time to halt and keep from crashing into him. He reached out and gripped her upper arms, keeping her from stumbling backwards, but the rapture in his expression was all she'd dreamed of minutes before. Nevertheless, the words he'd spoken when they'd last talked echoed in her memory, and she stepped out of his hold.

"What are you doing here?" The words came out on a brusque note, and Julia wished she could take them back almost as soon as they left her lips.

Seth stiffened, and the haze that had covered his mind at the sight of the vision in blue immediately lifted at her cool tone. How could she be so breathtaking and so aggravating, both at the same time? He had no business longing for a woman like Julia, even if they'd been headed toward something serious years ago. She was stunning and clearly out of his reach.

A pastor's wife should be modest in her dress and behavior. As soon as the thought entered he rejected it as low and unworthy. Julia had never been anything but modest and proper, regardless of the areas in town she chose to visit. He had no right to judge her behavior.

His only thought should be for her safety. Too much emphasis was already being placed on her by the well-meaning women of his congregation, and he would not add to that pressure.

"Forgive me for staring. It's been some time since I saw you so beautifully attired. As to my purpose here, I've come to give you a message from Mrs. Jacobs. She's been detained and will arrive soon. I happened to be calling on her husband when little Amanda took a spill from a chair."

"Oh my." Julia's fingers flew to her lips. "Is the child badly hurt?"

"Only her pride, from what I saw. Her knees were skinned, and she was in need of comfort, but I believe her older sister Lucy will see to her care once the ladies depart." Seth moved to the side to allow a finely clad man and woman to enter the dining room. The man bowed as he passed, and the woman gave a slight nod.

"I see. I wonder if I should return to my room or wait here." Julia cast a glance about the sitting area in the hotel foyer before returning her attention to him.

"I'd be happy to wait with you if you'd like."

Julia bit her lip but didn't reply.

Seth's heart plummeted. Apparently she was still irked with him for his comments last night.

He stiffened but didn't remove his gaze. "I have people to call on in town, so I'll bid you good-day, since it appears you would rather wait alone. I want you to know, Julia, that I meant what I said last night."

Julia's lips parted—she'd been so close to telling him to stay—to apologizing for not being more courteous, when he'd opened his mouth and ruined it all. "And so did I. Every word."

She had no desire to wait alone, but she wouldn't say so now, that was for sure. Couldn't he admit he might have made a mistake in judgment last night? Or did he truly believe she wasn't capable of taking care of herself?

She lifted her chin and pressed her lips together, trying to conceal her hurt. Either way, she could not let him see she wanted him to stay. "I do not plan to change my mind, either."

Seth extended his hand and grasped hers, allowing his fingers to linger. "Julia—please . . ."

Firm footfalls sounded on the thin carpet behind them, and Julia saw Seth's face smooth into neutral lines, but not before she'd noticed a hint of irritation. Surely he wouldn't feel so about Mrs. Jacobs and her guests? She swung around, and her spine stiffened.

Mrs. Evans stormed across the foyer toward them, her shoulders thrown back and nose pointing toward the ceiling. "Well, I never." She halted not three feet from Seth and scowled.

"Sparking a woman in public, Pastor? And with someone known to frequent unsavory places in town, no less. I see I may need to bring certain matters to the church elders, after all. This is quite unseemly. Quite. What do you have to say for yourself, sir?"

Julia stepped close to the woman, cutting off Seth's reply. "He has nothing to answer for, Mrs. Evans. He was not doing anything inappropriate—simply encouraging me to listen to his counsel."

She raised her brows and met Seth's eyes then turned her attention back to Mrs. Evans. "I appreciate the insight the pastor has shared, but I don't happen to agree with his opinion, so there's nothing more to be said. Now, I'll bid you both good day. It appears the people I am dining with have arrived."

She didn't so much as waste a glance on Mrs. Evans but spared a brief look in Seth's direction.

His firm lips and clenched jaw said it all. Her statement had accomplished its purpose—letting Mrs.

Evans know she had no interest in pursuing a relationship, and hopefully, making it clear to Seth she wouldn't listen to his concerns over where she went in this town.

It was important she make her own way and follow her own convictions. She didn't believe her safety was at risk, no matter what Seth said. After all, the only person in town who'd ever caused her any concern was Mrs. Evans.

Katherine Jacobs paused beside her mother and Mrs. Roberts, with Beth Roberts slightly behind, waiting as Julia walked unhurriedly across the hotel lobby. Each of the women were dressed in light-weight, modest day dresses, with full skirts and nicely fitted bodices.

Katherine wore blue, Mrs. Cooper in soft dove gray, Beth in a rich green that accented the color of her dark-brown hair hanging loose down the middle of her back, with Mrs. Roberts decked out in a slightly more gaudy, mauve creation with frills and poufs in quite unlikely places.

Julia smiled. The woman had seemed rather ostentatious on their first meeting, but she liked her all the same. Something about her brusque, but kind, personality drew and refreshed her.

Julia stepped closer. "I'm so glad you were able to come. Pastor Seth told me you were delayed. Is your daughter well?"

Katherine nodded, and a smile lit her beautiful face. "Yes, Mandy is quite resilient. It wasn't a bad spill, and her older sister Lucy is fussing over her with Zachary's help. I'm afraid Mandy might take another tumble off a chair in the future simply to repeat this special treatment."

Mrs. Cooper huffed, but one corner of her mouth twitched. "She had better not." She placed her palm over her heart. "The little dickens liked to have scared ten years off the short amount of life I have left on this earth."

Mrs. Roberts looped her hand through Mrs. Cooper's arm. "The child is fine. Amanda had nothing more than a skinned knee, and from what I've seen, Lucy and Zachary are more than capable of watching her. Mr. Tucker is working at the desk in the parlor, so I'm sure she'll be all right. Now let's go. I'm famished."

She patted her stomach and laughed. "Not that I couldn't do with losing a few pounds, but I'd hate to make anyone else feel uncomfortable by not eating."

Mrs. Cooper's brows rose, and she snorted. "I declare, Wilma. You do beat all. After breakfast you said you could not eat another bite all day, and now you are famished. If you truly want to lose a few pounds, take control of your appetite and resist the urge to eat."

Mrs. Roberts took a step back and swept her gaze down the full length of Mrs. Cooper's tiny frame. "You could never understand the needs of a larger woman, Frances, so please don't worry your head about what doesn't concern you. Now come along, all of you. The soup and biscuits here are divine, as is the pie."

Beth rolled her eyes and bit back a smile, but Julia saw her lips twitch as she followed the older women into the room. She fell into step beside the younger woman, glad to meet someone her own age. "Are they always so . . . contentious?" Julia leaned close and whispered, happy that the increased noise in the dining room kept her voice from drifting to the group ahead.

Beth giggled. "I'm afraid so, but they mean well. That wasn't the case when we first arrived in Baker City and moved to Mrs. Jacobs' boardinghouse. But Aunt Wilma and Mrs. Cooper have reconciled their differences—at least, most of the time.

"Much of what they say is good-natured bluster, so you mustn't let it distress you. I truly believe they enjoy their verbal sparring matches, but they view themselves as friends in spite of how it may appear."

"I see." Julia wasn't sure she did, but she let it pass. It wasn't like she'd be around the ladies much in the future. "I'm pleased Mrs. Jacobs invited me to luncheon. It was very kind." She bit her lip, wondering if she should say anything about rushing out of the church to the Lee family's aid.

Beth smiled and slowed her pace as they neared the table where the other three women were taking seats. "Please don't concern yourself with what women of Mrs. Evans' type think or say. There are people at the church who like you, and if she's not one of them, I hope you won't let it bother you."

Warmth spread through Julia's body, and the icy lump in her chest melted a tad. Beth had appeared quite shy and almost reticent the couple of times Julia had seen her, but she held her own quite well when one-on-one.

It would be nice to have a friend in town—someone who understood and whom she could confide in—but would any truly nice woman understand when she discovered Julia frequented the back alleys and saloons in town, seeking women to aid?

Beth stopped behind a chair and waited for Julia to slide out the one next to her, then withdrew her own and sat. "Aunt Wilma, Mrs. Cooper, Mrs. Jacobs—I have an idea. I do hope I'm not speaking out of turn, Mrs. Jacobs."

Frances gave an indulgent smile and nodded. "Since you rarely speak at all, my dear, I am sure whatever you have to say will be deemed quite suitable. I have always thought you did an admirable job in staying within the bounds of propriety. Amazing, considering the example you have had much of your life." She smirked at Wilma Roberts across the round table.

Mrs. Roberts sniffed. "I cannot believe you, Frances Cooper. Propriety indeed! I could name a time or two—"

Beth laid her fingers over her aunt's and squeezed. "Shh. You're allowing Mrs. Cooper to goad you again, Auntie, and it appears she's getting enjoyment from it, if her smile is any indication. Now let me say what I'd planned, all right?"

The older woman's spine relaxed, and she sank against her chair. "Of course, my dear. I apologize."

Beth's gaze lingered on Katherine Jacobs' face. "There's an empty room at the house. I can imagine it is expensive lodging at this hotel, even if a person were to pay by the month. Why not ask Miss McKenzie to move in with us? We'd enjoy her company, I'm sure, and it would save her money. What do you all think?"

Julia stifled a gasp, wishing she could disappear from the table, if not the room. She'd had no idea Beth would suggest such a thing, and no matter how appealing it might be, she didn't want Mrs. Jacobs or the others to feel they must fall in with the younger woman's enthusiastic suggestion.

She lifted a hand. "Please. Don't worry on my behalf. It's a very sweet suggestion, but . . ." But what? She had ample funds? She didn't care for their company?

What excuse could she possibly give? Most people would love to move from a hotel to a cozy boardinghouse. Not that she'd seen the home in question, but if these ladies lived there, it must be more than acceptable.

Katherine met her gaze and smiled. "Nonsense. I don't know why I didn't think of it myself. It's a lovely idea. You must come. Unless you don't want to. If you've paid in advance here, I imagine they'd give you a refund." The other three women chimed in, their voices blending together in enthusiastic accord.

Julia looked from one to the other, her heart in her throat. She'd almost grasped at the invitation—almost said yes, when the truth hit her. How could she slip out of the house in the wee hours when the girls were headed home from the saloons, without the other residents knowing?

Surely they must have rules about not leaving in the middle of the night unless it was an emergency. Even if they didn't, would they understand?

More than likely they'd say the same things Seth had said—it was dangerous, she was foolish, or worse, they'd start gawking as Mrs. Evans and her sort did.

Julia worked hard to smile, but it died on her lips at the sight of the four expectant faces around the table. "I don't quite know what to say, other than thank you."

Beth beamed. "So you'll come? I can help you pack if you'd like."

Julia shook her head. "I need time to think about it. It's not that I don't appreciate it, but there are things I must consider." She bit her lip.

Beth's warm glow faded. "Are you worried they'll withhold the money you've paid? Possibly Pastor Seth or Mr. Jacobs could speak to the manager if you feel it might be a problem."

"No, it's not that." She closed her eyes for a brief moment, working to gather her thoughts. "It's a lovely suggestion, and I might take you up on it, but I'd like a few days to decide. Would that be all right, Mrs. Jacobs, or do you require a decision now?"

Katherine smiled. "If I have someone inquire about the room in the next day or so, I'll send word and let you know. Otherwise, you may take whatever time you need."

The waitress arrived and stopped by their table. The voices faded and Julia's stomach knotted. More than anything she'd like to be friends with this group of women, but she wouldn't give up her mission for anyone.

Chapter Six

Julia stepped out of the front door of the hotel and perused the night sky, wishing the full moon would peek out from behind the heavy bank of clouds. It hadn't been this dark on any of the previous nights she'd gone to check on her girls, as she'd come to think of some of the young women who'd felt driven to accept work at some of the more unsavory places in town.

She shivered and pulled her shawl closer. Apprehension pricked at her spine as Seth's warning came to mind. She almost pivoted to dash back to her room, but stopped herself in time. What nonsense to be fearful. No man in his right mind would harm a decent woman on the streets of this city, even if it was after midnight.

She crossed her arms over her chest and rubbed her upper arms, trying to rid herself of a sudden chill. How about a drunken man? Maybe it would be best to avoid the front of the saloon tonight.

Stepping off the boardwalk, she struck out across the street, thankful for the lack of traffic that usually streamed past. Diagonally and one block down, raucous music blared from the open saloon doors. Light streamed out, and Julia made out the dark form of a man staggering across the boardwalk toward a horse tied at the rail.

She paused. She'd assumed that midnight was early enough not to encounter anyone going home, but late enough to check on the women who often slipped into the back alley for a break after long hours on the job.

The man swung unsteadily into the saddle, then turned his horse away from where she stood and headed up the street. Julia relaxed and took a deep breath, her heart thumping. She'd never been apprehensive before Seth planted the seed of worry in her mind about her safety, and she'd never had anyone so much as approach her in a way that wasn't appropriate.

Shaking off her fear, she eased forward, thankful for the deep dust that masked the sound of her footfalls—although worrying over that seemed foolish with the amount of noise coming from the saloon.

A block from the front door, Julia turned a corner and increased her pace. It was later than she'd ever arrived, and any girl hoping to talk or share a concern might have given up by now.

An edge of the moon slipped out from behind the clouds, casting a sliver of light on her path, but the bulk of the alley was still cloaked in darkness.

Julia's step faltered as she reached the midway point. Sickness assailed her belly. What was she doing here? The best she'd been able to do was give a coin here and there when needed, or patch up a bruised or battered body.

Mei was the only one who'd embraced the concept of a relationship with God—and Mei wasn't even on duty tonight. But other women had acted as though they appreciated the help she offered, even if none of them had chosen to leave this life. She needed to keep praying, keep working, keep trusting that God would reach these women and show them the way to a better existence.

She surged determinedly toward the alley entrance, then slowed. Something wasn't right. Squaring her shoulders, she pushed the warning away. What if she sensed a woman in need? Someone might be hurt, or even dying from a beating. Not once in the past had she experienced fear of any kind, much less the desire to bolt back to the hotel.

Striking out again, she kept her chin high and her focus on the shadowy figure of a woman a few yards ahead. At least one girl had waited. Satisfaction filled Julia's heart. Her determination to overcome her dread had proven to be the right decision—perhaps she could make a difference in at least one life tonight.

Seth prowled the front porch of the house he occupied only a stone's throw from the church. Something was wrong, but he had no idea what it might be. He'd been awakened from a deep sleep to an awareness of danger. He'd jerked on his clothes as quickly as possible then dashed out the door ready to defend whoever might be in need.

He'd skidded to a halt before he reached the edge of his porch. "What should I do, Lord?" He raised his face to the dark sky.

He couldn't skulk around the streets looking for someone in need when he had no idea where to go or if this forewarning was true. He shot up another quick prayer for guidance, then headed back inside.

Seth grabbed the lantern hanging on a hook behind the door and set it on the table, then he fumbled around in a box of matches and lit the wick. What he wouldn't give for this town to have the new-fangled gaslights the newspapers boasted about in the big cities back east.

He shrugged on a coat then held the lantern high, stepping off the porch and heading up the road toward the center of town. A memory surged of Julia wandering around in the alley behind one of the saloons the first day he saw her.

After he'd warned her to be careful and stay in her hotel at night, he hoped she wasn't the cause of his alarm, but he couldn't quiet his unease. After all, the stubborn woman had insisted she'd do as she pleased.

Julia drew closer to what appeared to be a woman standing with her head tipped down. "Are you all right, miss? Is there anything I can do to help?"

Suddenly, what she'd thought was the form of a woman turned into a man wearing long, shaggy hair who stepped out from behind a discarded whiskey barrel, giving the illusion of a wide skirt. He raised his head just as the clouds parted the rest of the way from the face of the moon, casting its light on his face.

A leering grin covered his visage, and he took another step toward her. "I ain't no woman, but you surely can help me. I was waitin' out here hopin' one of them saloon girls would come to visit. They tossed me outta there when I run out of money, and I didn't get a chance to socialize with any of them girls."

He drew closer and grabbed Julia's wrist. "You'll do right fine instead."

As the man jerked her up against his filthy shirt, Julia could smell the stench of liquor on his breath. She emitted a piercing scream and yanked her arm free, then kicked his shin hard and turned to flee.

"Oh no you don't, missy. You come in here of your own accord, and I don't aim to let you leave yet. No ma'am." He jumped forward and wrapped his arm around her waist then spun her to face him again, lowering his face to hers.

Quickening his walk, Seth rounded a corner at the end of the business district, wondering where to begin. Maybe a miner or cowboy was in trouble, possibly someone who'd had too much to drink. Tinny piano music drifted from the open doors of the saloon, and Seth headed in that direction.

He stopped a few yards in front of the entrance, waiting. For what? Someone to stumble outside? That happened all the time in this town. What did God want of him, anyway?

He pivoted and took one stride forward when a woman's scream rent the air, coming from somewhere behind the building. He took off at a run, wishing the saloon was situated closer to the end of the block rather than the middle. At this rate, he might be too late to help whoever was in distress.

Julia struggled and screamed again, barely turning her head in time to miss his slobbering lips as they landed close to her ear. "Let go of me, you lout! I'm not a saloon girl, and I want nothing to do with you." She clawed at what felt like strong bands gripping her, but the man didn't loosen his hold.

"You should'a thought of that before you came traipsin' into this alley. No honest woman would be out at this time of night."

He gave a hoarse cough of laughter. "Now you're gonna give me a little kiss to pay me for my time. Then we can talk a while, and maybe mosey on over to wherever you live after that." He grabbed a handful of hair and tipped her head back, then nuzzled her neck.

Julia's stomach roiled, and her vision darkened at the same time her knees started to weaken. She'd never fainted in her life, but she couldn't stand much more of this manhandling.

Suddenly, the man released her and Julia flew backwards as though wrenched from his grip by a powerful force. She landed against the clapboard wall of the saloon, smacking so hard bolts of pain shot up her spine.

As her vision and focus returned, Julia pushed herself upright and took in the scene unfolding before her. By the light of a lantern perched on the top of a barrel, she witnessed the man who had assaulted her dive at Seth, arms flailing. Seth swung his fist and connected with the ruffian's chin, knocking him to the ground.

The man rolled to one side, grunted, and pushed up on his knee, then staggered to his feet and backed away from Seth.

"You got no call to hit me, mister. That woman came here on her own. I didn't drag her. She should'a known some man would want a kiss or two, her comin' here all pretty and sassy."

He swiped blood streaming from a cut in the corner of his lips and then spat. "I got no quarrel with you."

Plucking his hat off the top of the barrel where he'd set it earlier, he dusted it against his leg. "If this is your woman, you'd best rein her in and make her stay at home where she belongs, a'fore some man has his way with her." He swung around and stalked down the alley.

Julia's thoughts churned, unable to grasp what she was feeling or thinking. She turned slowly toward Seth, then she bolted forward, unable to conquer the shaking that gripped her body.

He opened his arms wide as she approached and gathered her close. Julia pressed her face against his chest and felt the wild galloping of his heart. He must have been almost as frightened as she, but he wasn't shaking. She held still, drawing strength from his embrace, thankful beyond measure that he'd somehow found her before it was too late.

Something touched her hair—light and gentle, but it sent a tremor through her body. He must have touched her hair with his fingertips. No. That wasn't possible. His arms were clasped around her, and he hadn't moved an inch. There it was again. She looked up in time to see him lifting his lips from her hair.

Warmth coursed into Julia's cheeks, bringing sudden awareness of her position. "You're hurt. He hit you." She pulled out of his embrace, and Seth dropped his arms.

He dabbed at his nose and gave a wry smile. "It's only a bloody nose. Nothing broken."

He stepped closer and clasped her hand, then picked up his lantern from the ground where he'd set it with his other. "And you? I saw you hit the wall hard, but I was occupied and couldn't help you to your feet when you fell."

Julia shivered and gripped his fingers, thankful for the warmth and comfort of his touch. "It's throbbing but not bad. I'm so sorry, Seth, that I caused trouble for you. I truly thought I was safe. No one has ever bothered me before, although this is the latest I've been out."

She loosened her hold and rubbed her arms. "Maybe that's the problem. I'll make sure I never come here close to midnight again."

Seth stared at Julia, barely able to comprehend her words. He'd been sick with fright when he'd rounded the corner and spotted the woman he cared for in that ruffian's clutches. When he'd held her and felt her soft form modeled against his in what seemed like total surrender, he'd hoped Julia had finally come to her senses and would allow him to keep her safe in the future.

But from the sound of things, that wasn't the case. "That was an incredibly foolish thing to do, Julia." His teeth clenched as the image of Julia in danger came back full force.

Now that he knew she was safe, Seth's body began to shake as anger bubbled to the surface. "You could have been killed tonight—or worse."

He faced her, grasping her arms and giving her a little shake. "Are you even listening to me? I can't believe you came to this part of town after dark. What if God hadn't awakened me and caused me to come? Do you realize what could have happened?"

The dim light of a lantern hung on a nail nearby shone on Julia's tear-wet face as she raised her chin and gave a slight nod. "Yes. I do now. I don't blame you for being angry."

He loosened his hold. "Don't you think it would be wiser to not come at all?"

"I might consider not coming at night, but I can't stop my work, Seth. That's what brought me to Baker City. I heard about the large population of Chinese. I knew they'd be shunned, if not mistreated, and many of their women work in the saloons. No one even sees those girls as people with needs. They could be beaten and tossed out for dead and nobody would care." Her gaze probed his, lingered, and her words ended with a slight sob.

Seth saw raw pain mixed with something else—something akin to fear. "What drives you, Julia? Why the Chinese?"

He tucked her hand into the crook of his elbow. "Let's walk. We don't want to stay here any longer." He guided her around the empty whiskey barrel and toward the end of the alley. "I've never understood what drew you to Baker City."

He wished Julia would say she'd learned he was here—that she'd longed to find him after so many years and had stumbled upon his location—but somehow he knew that wasn't the case. After all, he hadn't tried to pursue her when she'd left so abruptly, so why think she might have searched for him, especially after so many years had passed?

But he'd been convinced she didn't care. The note she'd left had been abrupt—without a hint of caring. Surely she wouldn't have wanted him traipsing after her and trying to bring her home?

Julia tightened her grip on his arm as they rounded the corner leading onto the main street. "My father hired a Chinese cook after my mother's death—you might remember her, although she rarely came out of the kitchen. Wu Sung had been badly beaten as a child, then when she was no longer pretty, her parents sold her as household help."

Julia glanced up at him, and Seth's steps slowed at the depth of anguish in her words. "She came to us a few years later and stayed with me when I left the parsonage after Papa's death. One night I got sick, and Sung insisted on going out to find medicine. She didn't come back that night, or the next day, nor the following one."

Seth's stomach clenched at what he thought might be coming. "What happened?"

"She made it home three days later, barely alive. A man had dragged her to a brothel housed in a saloon. They told her that was all the Chinese women were good for, and she needed to learn her place. She was beaten and abused, and if it hadn't been for the kindness of a white woman, she wouldn't have gotten free."

He felt a shiver course through her body. "When I told the police, they laughed and asked what I thought they should do about it. They claimed she went there of her own free will, and there was nothing illegal about working at the saloon. They shooed us away like we were dung under their feet."

"Where is Sung now?" Seth wanted to stop and wrap his arms around Julia again and pull her close but something stopped him. She needed to talk—she'd probably wanted to share this story for years, and he couldn't interrupt. The telling might free something inside that had been damaged and bruised and caused her to act the way she did now.

She dropped her head and sniffed. "She died. I used some of the money from Mama's jewelry to bury her, but they wouldn't let me place her near Papa. She had to be buried in a Chinese burial plot on the outskirts of town. It was awful the way she died, Seth."

Julia lifted her face, and tears streamed down her cheeks. "I swore right then that I'd do everything in my power to protect women like her. She didn't ask for that treatment. Sung was a good, decent woman who loved me. *No man* has the right to treat a woman that way—I don't care what color they are—and I won't stop trying to help any woman who needs to find a better life."

Seth stopped and gripped Julia's shoulder. "Don't you see? The same thing almost happened to you tonight. I know you care about these women, and so do I. But you can't continue to risk your life. That's not going to change their plight. Let others do this. Promise me, Julia."

She pulled away. "Don't ask me that, Seth. Please. Of all people, I thought you'd understand. I know you care about my safety, but there are things more important in this world than one's self."

Chapter Seven

Julia slid into the seat at the Arlington Hotel Restaurant and smiled at Wilma Roberts, who'd arrived prior to her. "It was so kind of you to come on short notice, Mrs. Roberts. I need someone to talk to, although I doubt you'll be glad you came when I finish. I'm not sure why I even asked you, except somehow you remind me of my father's sister who's no longer with us."

She bit her lip, afraid she'd blurted out too much and might be in danger of scaring this woman away.

Mrs. Roberts' mouth quirked in a gentle smile. "I came as much for myself as for you, Miss McKenzie. My niece and I haven't met a lot of people in Baker City and have very few friends since arriving. And I want you to call me Wilma. I get quite enough of 'Mrs. Roberts' at the boardinghouse."

She placed her forearms on the table and leaned forward. "Now, would you like to continue with a few minutes of polite conversation, or would you prefer to get right to what's bothering you?"

Julia gaped, then composed herself and chuckled. "My. You are forthright. I must say I appreciate it. I'd love to jump right in, if you don't feel I'm being too bold. And if you don't mind, please call me Julia."

Wilma nodded. "That sounds lovely. You aren't being bold, at all. I wouldn't have offered had I not meant it." She waved her fingers in the air. "I'll try not to interrupt."

"Thank you." Julia linked her hands together on the tabletop and drew in a shaky breath, wondering yet again if she'd made a rash decision when she'd contacted this woman. "I've been thinking about taking up Katherine's offer of moving to her boardinghouse."

Wilma thumped her palm against the table. "That's wonderful news! I can't see why you'd be apprehensive— in fact, you should have come to the house and talked to Katherine. Better yet, how about I help you pack and we'll go together?"

"Wait." Julia shivered, hating that Wilma had gotten the wrong idea. "I'm afraid you don't understand. After you hear everything, you might not feel I should come."

Wilma started to speak again but halted when Julia frowned. "You were at the church the evening the little Chinese boy came for help, and you saw me run after him. I'm sure you also noticed how unhappy Mrs. Evans and a couple of other women were, that Pastor Seth came as well."

"Yes, but what does that have to do ..." She stopped again. "I'm sorry. Go ahead. I'll try to simply listen."

"It's fine, really. I don't mind if you have something to say. But it might be easier if I could get things off my mind before we have a discussion."

A waiter paused at their table carrying a tray with a shiny silver pot. "Would you ladies care for coffee, or should I bring tea? Anything else you'd like to order? Our pie is especially good today."

Wilma smiled. "Coffee is fine, thank you, but nothing else."

Julia gave her assent too, and waited for the waiter to pour and then depart. "As I was saying, you noticed me leave with Meng, the little Chinese boy. What you don't know is that's not the first time I've visited their community. In fact, I spend a lot of time in Meng's home, as well as . . . other places."

Wilma took a sip of from her cup. "Such as?"

Julia relaxed a tiny bit as she searched Wilma's face and saw no hint of censure. "I also frequent the saloons." The air whooshed out of her lungs as she realized how that sounded. "Not in the saloons—outside them— behind them, actually. Oh my gracious, this is not coming out the way I wanted it to."

The older woman reached across the table and clasped her hand, gave it a light squeeze and released her. "Try again, slower this time. I'm not in a hurry. And believe me when I tell you that you picked the right person when it comes to not judging someone for their actions or their past."

"Thank you." Julia slipped her hands into her lap, embarrassed that Wilma had witnessed her discomfort.

"I don't frequent the saloons. I go there hoping to minister to the women who work there, regardless of their color. Most of them are not in that life by choice. They've been abandoned with no way of making a living, or circumstances have forced them into that lifestyle. The Chinese are treated like possessions by the saloon owners, even more so than the white women. It's truly despicable, and so few people, even within the church, care to rectify the situation."

Wilma gave a slow nod, her brows drawn. "I understand what you're saying, but do you believe that the average genteel person would understand how to approach women who've made the choice to work there, whatever the reason? I know I wouldn't, and life has not treated me kindly, in many regards."

She drew in a quiet breath. "I imagine that most church members, even true Christians, don't feel themselves equipped to brave the dens of iniquity, as they'd see a saloon, even to the saving of a soul. Is it right that we judge them harshly, because they fail at something that even most preachers would hesitate to tackle?"

Julia leaned forward as emotion surged to the forefront. She had to work to keep her tone even and her voice down, lest other patrons in the restaurant notice.

"But that's the thing. Don't you believe a pastor should be the first person to tackle injustice? To speak against it from the pulpit and go out into the streets, hoping to effect a change? Why should it be a woman who takes up this cross, when a pastor is supposed to be called to gather the sheep who have gone astray?"

Her companion sat quietly for several moments, as though considering Julia's words. Then she lifted her chin. "Is the woman called to take up this particular cross?"

Julia sat as though anchored to her chair. "Well, yes. I suppose she is, if by the woman you mean me."

Wilma nodded. "What is the pastor's calling, do you suppose?"

Julia searched for the meaning behind Wilma's question. "I assume it would be to reach people with the gospel, but doesn't that include the downtrodden and abused, as well as those who attend the church?"

Wilma laced her fingers around her coffee cup and lifted it to her mouth, then set it on the saucer again. "Yes, I'm certain it would include them all. But I was asking about a pastor's specific calling."

"I'm sorry. I'm not following."

"Is every woman called to visit the alleyways behind the saloon, in hopes of ministering to fallen women? Or even to attend the Chinese people in their homes? Am I a sinner, or less of a Christian than you, because my ministry might be to aid someone other than those you feel drawn to help?" Her words were even and calm, but nonetheless, they dug deep.

Julia winced. "I wasn't pointing my finger at you."

"Ah, but weren't you?" Wilma leaned forward, her expression soft and kind, almost giving lie to her direct words. "I'm sure you didn't think of it that way, but aren't you judging others for what you perceive as their sin of not caring?

Julia, this is *your* calling—*your* ministry—something *you* are passionate about. I see that in your eyes and hear it in your voice—in the very way you hold yourself—you love these people with every fiber of your being."

Julia stared at Wilma, working to comprehend. At first, it seemed the older woman was chastising her, but then it appeared she could see into the very core of Julia's heart. "Yes, I do love them, and I want to help in any way possible."

"And that's admirable. In fact, you should follow what God has called you to do. Let's take Pastor Seth, for example."

Julia tried not to wince. More than once she'd been frustrated with Seth's seeming lack of awareness for the plight of the broken and fallen women in town, even while she was attracted and drawn to him as a man. He'd helped Meng's father when the older man was injured and never once complained. But would he have done it on his own, if she hadn't been involved?

"Julia?"

"Yes. I'm sorry."

Wilma settled back in her chair, her gaze dark and compelling. "Has it occurred to you that Pastor Seth might have his own ministry, apart from what you think it should be?"

"Like preaching every Sunday."

"More than that. You know Micah Jacobs, Katherine's husband?"

"Yes. I've met him a couple of times."

"Were you aware he was antagonistic toward God and the church when he arrived in Baker City?"

Julia started, unsure she'd heard correctly. "I find that hard to envision. The man is active in the church and appears to love God very much."

"Yes, now he does. But that's because Seth reached out to him after a near tragedy and broke through his hard shell. He got the entire town involved in restoring Micah's belief in God and man. I truly am not sure anyone else could have done what he did, right when Micah was at the deepest point of his need. In fact, I don't believe Micah and Katherine would be married now, had it not been for Seth's intervention."

"So, you're saying Seth doesn't *have to* care about the women in town, or the drunks, or the Chinese, because he helps people like Mr. Jacobs?" Julia leaned back and crossed her arms as frustration poured over her. It was all well and good what Seth had accomplished, but that didn't address her question.

"Not at all. What I mean is that God places different burdens on each heart. Can you imagine if every single Christian and pastor had the same calling? What would happen to all the other needs in the world—or even in this town, for that matter? God calls all of us in a unique way. As none of us are created identically in appearance or how we think, or feel, we're also not given the same gifts.

We must be responsible for where God plants us, rather than judge others for not being in the same place. That's not to say that our calling can't change, or we might see a hardship and strive to fix it. But if we don't, then we're accountable to God, rather than to one another. Does that make sense?"

Julia nodded. She heaved a deep sigh then unclasped her arms and braced them on the table. "I believe it does. I've been hurt and angry at Christians for a long time— ever since my father's congregation abandoned me and cast me out of our home after his death."

Wilma gripped Julia's hand again. "There is no excuse for that kind of behavior, and I'm so sorry it happened. But not forgiving leads to deep-rooted anger and bitterness and will poison the one holding onto it, much more than the person it's directed towards. Besides, what your father's congregation did isn't the same thing as this church or Pastor Seth not meeting the needs of the fallen women in town. You see that, don't you?"

"Yes, I suppose I do. I didn't before. I lumped them all into the same pot."

Wilma squeezed Julia's fingers and smiled. "The only way to true healing and freedom is by forgiving those who have hurt you."

Julia sat up straight and leaned back. "The people at church never asked for my forgiveness, nor acknowledged their wrong. If I forgive them, then I'm saying what they did was all right. I won't forgive the man who beat and abused Sung, either. None of them deserve forgiveness, and I do not intend to grant it."

"Someday, I'll share my niece's story with you, but not today." The sad cloud on Wilma's face cleared, and she smiled. "Suffice it to say, I understand what you're saying more than you realize. Let me ask you a question, and I want you to think carefully before you respond. Did you deserve the forgiveness Jesus provided?"

Julia sucked in her breath, ready to give a quick answer, then paused. "But I didn't abandon someone I should have taken care of, nor did I beat a helpless woman until she died. I'm neither a criminal nor a terrible person. I may not have deserved forgiveness, but I did nothing of which to be ashamed." She winced. "But I know I'm not perfect."

"None of us are. He alone is righteous. Holy. But He loved us enough to send His son to earth."

"I know all of this. My father was a pastor, remember?" Julia tried to stifle her irritation, but she knew it must show in her face and voice. "I'm sorry. You're right. I've done things I'm not proud of, even if they aren't huge. But if I forgive those people, it's like I'm saying what they did to me and to Sung doesn't matter."

"No. It simply shows you're putting it into God's control. He's the only one who can rightfully judge our sins. But if you continue to hold onto your wrath—if you refuse to forgive—then you tie God's hands."

Wilma laid her fingertips over her heart. "He wants to set you free from the bitterness and pain you've been carrying, but He can't as long as you hold onto the hurt. Forgiving isn't saying what they did is right, it's simply letting go of the past and choosing to walk toward God's light and love, instead of toward darkness."

"If I ever go back home, I'll have nothing to do with those people." Unease rose up in Julia at the thought, leaving her almost physically ill.

Wilma shook her head, her face serious. "God doesn't require we be friends with those who hurt us or even return to a previous relationship. That's not to say you couldn't be courteous should you meet one of the church members on the street, but forgiveness doesn't necessitate friendship. Sometimes it even requires a separation from the person, for our own safety, and that's as it should be."

Julia eased back against her chair. "Thank you," she whispered. "Thank you for listening. For caring. You're the first person I've ever completely opened up to—at least, to this degree. I had no idea how much this had poisoned my attitude toward other Christians. I know what you said is true, and I will think deeply on it."

Wilma gave a gentle nod. "Good. I'll be praying for you as you consider our conversation. And will you move to the boardinghouse now?" Her face broke into a genuine smile.

"Do you think Katherine and her husband would want me, knowing what I feel called to do?"

"Ministering to the women and the Chinese? Of course they would. They are both decent, loving people. Even if they aren't drawn to do the same, they've reached out to other people in their own way, within the confines of their home and at the church."

Julia nodded. "I've decided not to go out at night anymore. Something convinced me recently that it's not a wise idea. But I won't quit visiting Mei and her family in Chinatown, or trying to help the women at the saloon."

"Humph! No one will ask you to, my dear. As long as you're careful and don't take foolish chances, I can't imagine it being an issue." Wilma's eyes twinkled. "Now, let's go gather your things. I brought the buggy just in case."

Julia rose and plucked her reticule from the back of her chair. Wilma might not think visiting Mei's family or the other women would become an issue, but after what happened in the alley, she wasn't so sure Seth would understand if she continued her mission—whether it be daytime or night.

Chapter Eight

Seth stopped at the desk in the lobby of the Arlington Hotel and waited impatiently for the clerk to turn from his task of sorting papers. Finally, Seth could wait no longer and cleared his throat. "Excuse me, I need to see one of your guests."

The clerk swiveled around and pushed his spectacles up onto the bridge of his nose and peered over the top of the rim. "And who might that be, sir?"

"Miss Julia McKenzie. Would you be able to send someone to her room and give her this note?" He held out the envelope containing the letter he'd spent the morning preparing and waited, tapping his toe to try to still his impatience.

"McKenzie? Hmm. Let me see." The clerk ignored the proffered envelope and turned his back on Seth to examine the wall of keys, then turned his attention to a ledger perched on the shelf below.

"McKenzie. McKenzie. Ah. Here we are." He ran his finger along a line near the bottom of the page and then faced Seth. "She checked out over three hours ago, sir."

The wind left Seth's lungs as if he'd been kicked by a heavily shod mule intent on doing serious damage. It took him a moment to regain his composure and speak.

"Three hours, you say? Did she leave word where she might be found? Another hotel, perhaps?"

The clerk's brows drew together. "No, sir. She said she'd send someone for her trunk, but she took the rest of her things. Nothing more. Is there anything else, sir?" He cast a glance over Seth's shoulder at a party of noisy men who'd entered the lobby.

"If you're certain she didn't give you her destination, then no. Thank you." He half-turned then swung back. "What time is her trunk being retrieved?"

The clerk pulled out a pocket watch and stared at it and then tucked it back into his vest. "I believe she said around four-thirty, which would be in a quarter of an hour. Now if you don't mind, I need to help these gentlemen."

Seth stepped to the side as three rough-clad miners moved up to the counter. This hotel drew everyone from the hard-working miners to prosperous business men— and the occasional lady like Julia. His heart pinched so tight it sent physical pain shooting through his chest.

Where could she have gone? Had she left the hotel on his account? Maybe he'd been too hard on her when he'd urged her to see to her safety above the needs of the Chinese women. But that was the right thing to advise her, wasn't it? It was his job—and the place of men like him to care for the hurting and abused of society, rather than the place of the respectable women in town.

Respectable women? He sank into a chair in the spacious lobby, almost blind to the people coming and going, appalled at the direction his thoughts had taken. When had he come to the point, even in his thoughts, of disparaging the women who worked in the saloons or the Chinese who waited on others so selflessly?

He was a pastor—a servant of God—and of the people—*all* the people, not only the ones who chose to attend his church or who were smiled on by others in the community.

In fact, if anything, he should be the pastor to the very same people Julia felt called to help. Why had it taken the selfless act of a brave woman for him to see that fact?

The urge to find Julia and share this newfound truth drove him from his chair. He stood in the lobby, staring around him, wondering where he should go. A cold wave washed over him. The stage had left town two hours ago. But why wouldn't Julia have taken her trunk?

And even more, would she have left without telling him goodbye? They hadn't parted on terrible terms last night—at least, not in his mind.

Seth bolted toward the front door. Julia was beautiful, and he doubted she could have purchased a ticket and boarded the stage without someone remembering.

He got as far as the door and paused, indecision warring inside. If he waited for the man who came to pick up the trunk, more than likely he'd end up following him to the stage station, regardless. He swung open the door and catapulted through it.

"Hey!" A pair of firm hands gripped him and pushed him back. "Slow down there, Seth. You about knocked me two-ways-to-Sunday." Micah Jacobs released him and grinned. "Now what's your hurry?"

"Sorry about that, Micah. I'm on my way to the stage station and in something of a rush."

"Hold it." Micah grabbed him as Seth tried to brush past. He pulled Seth out of the way of a man entering the door and moved over to the wall of the hotel. "You catching the stage out of town? Who's going to speak on Sunday? Mind telling me what's going on?"

Seth clamped his teeth together and bit back an impatient retort. This wasn't like him, but right now he didn't care. He had to find out where Julia had gone, before it was too late.

"The stage left a couple of hours ago, so I'm not going—yet. I need to find out where Miss McKenzie went after she checked out of the hotel. The only place I can figure is she boarded the stage and maybe headed home."

A sly grin creased Micah's face, and he gave a short nod. "So that's the way the wind blows, is it? I guess I should'a seen it coming."

"Seen what coming? Quit talking in riddles, man. In fact, if you want to talk to me at all, you'd better walk while you do, because I'm going to the stage station right now." He shook off Micah's grip and took one stride, only to be halted again by the man's firm grasp.

"Whoa, there. You didn't give me a chance to finish what I started to say. There's no need to ask at the stage station. I can tell you where she went."

Hope bubbled in Seth's chest, but almost as quickly subsided. Knowing where she went wouldn't bring her back. "To Omaha? Back home?"

Micah shook his head. "I didn't even know she was from Omaha. Nope. She's out at our place sipping tea with the ladies as we speak. Although hopefully a few of them will be getting supper on the table by the time I get back with Miss McKenzie's trunk." He clapped Seth on the back with a hard thump. "Feel better now?"

Seth's jaw slackened. "Your house? Not to the stage?" He closed his mouth and swallowed hard, then grinned. "Yeah. I think I do. Any chance you might have room for one more at your table tonight?"

Julia sat on the bed in her room at the boardinghouse and closed the Bible. Where had all those verses on forgiveness come from that had seemed to jump out at her for the past hour? She remembered some from her childhood, but it seemed like the others had been placed there especially for her.

Everything Wilma had said fell into place. All these years, she'd been poisoning herself with her anger and resentment. Her lack of forgiveness hadn't affected the people who'd wronged her in the slightest—if anything, according to what she'd read, her lack of trusting God with the situation might even have kept Him from dealing with them.

Well, no more. It was time to let it all go. She bowed her head and waited, but felt nothing. "God?" She lifted her face toward heaven. "I guess You'll have to help me with this. I don't feel like forgiving any of those people, but I'm going to be obedient and do it because I know I should. And I do choose to, Lord. I hope that's good enough, because right now, it's all I can offer."

She closed her eyes and waited, hoping she'd hear His voice in some quiet way. Instead, a deep peace washed over her spirit, and the tension flowed from her body, leaving her more relaxed and at ease than she'd felt in years. Could it really be as simple as taking a step of obedience and agreeing to forgive, whether her emotions were involved or not? It certainly seemed so.

"I give it all to You. Everything that I don't understand. And please, forgive me for my resentment against You, against other Christians, and even against Seth. I was so wrong, and I'm sorry."

Another wave of deep, soothing peace flooded her heart, and she sighed. "Thank you, Father, so very much." She sat for several more minutes, drinking in the new sense of calm and wellbeing.

She wished she'd realized it could be so easy—while at the same time, it had been hard. But it had been years since she'd dug into her Bible, and even longer since she'd done so with any real desire to learn.

A tap on her door startled her, and she jumped from the bed. "Yes? Who's there?"

"It's Lucy, Miss McKenzie. Ma said to tell you it's suppertime."

"Thank you. I'll be right down." She stepped to the oval mirror above the bureau then turned the wick up higher on the lamp. A curl or two out of place, but otherwise presentable enough for the gathering of family and boarders.

She appeared tired, with tiny puffs below her eyes. At least she'd sleep well tonight and hopefully look better before she encountered Seth again.

Seth—she hadn't told him she'd moved. Her hand flew to her throat. What would he think if he came to the hotel for some reason? But surely he wouldn't. There wasn't any reason for him to check on her or to call. Maybe she could go into town tomorrow and leave word at the church so he wouldn't worry.

She straightened her skirt and then opened the door. It was time to eat and trust that everything else would somehow fall into place.

When she arrived at the dining room door, the amiable chatter at the table ceased and everyone turned her way, but she only saw one face. Seth Russell sat at the far end across from the only other empty place.

Her heart hammered so fast she thought it would break right through her chest. Why was Seth here—she hadn't made enough of an effort with her appearance— she must go back to her room and try again.

She did a half turn then paused. Wait. More than likely Seth was here on a pastoral call to someone in the family. It was sheer foolishness to assume he'd come to see her.

Seth rose out of his chair and the rest of the men almost fell over their chairs to stand, apparently following his lead. "Julia. You are lovely." His voice cracked on the last word and he cleared his throat, but he remained standing, a worried smile trembling on his lips.

Frances Cooper waved her fingers. "My gracious, gentlemen. None of you jump to your feet when *I* enter a room. Sit, please, so we can get on with our supper." Her brows rose as all the men sat except Seth.

"Pastor, would you care to sit and join us for supper?"

Wilma Roberts tsked. "Now, Frances, there's no call for sarcasm. Leave the boy alone. Can't you see he's happy to see Miss McKenzie?"

Frances smirked. "Unless I am greatly mistaken, I would say he is that and more, Wilma, dear."

Katherine clicked her spoon against her water glass. "Ladies, let's not embarrass Pastor Seth or Miss McKenzie any further. Julia, you may take the place beside Lucy."

Katherine smiled and waited until Julia took her place. "I'm not sure if you've met everyone, Miss McKenzie." She nodded to a handsome young man Julia had noticed at church.

"This is Mr. Jeffery Tucker, a novelist. You know my husband and children, and you've met my mother, Mrs. Cooper, Beth Roberts and her aunt, Mrs. Roberts, when we took luncheon together."

"It's nice to see you all." Julia spread her napkin on her lap and glanced at Katherine. "I'm glad you have room for me."

Wilma's brows rose. "No need for the formality with me, Katherine. Remember, Julia and I took tea together earlier today. We've become quite good friends." She shot a triumphant smirk across the table at Frances.

Katherine rolled her eyes, but a smile touched her lips. "Now ladies, let's not worry about who's friends with whom right now. Micah, would you please bless the food?"

Thirty minutes later, Julia's hands shook as she folded her napkin and laid it beside her plate. She'd barely eaten a bite since she'd taken her place across from Seth. Other than his initial reaction when she'd entered the room, he'd acted as though nothing was wrong, smiling and joking with the men. He didn't act angry or upset.

She longed to talk to him and at least share a small part of what she'd decided while speaking with Wilma.

Finally, Julia could stand it no longer. She waited until a number of people were conversing, then leaned forward, directing her attention at him. "Pastor Russell, is this an official call in your duty as clergy?"

His brows rose, but he didn't flinch. "No, Miss McKenzie. I was hoping to have a few minutes of your time this evening."

Her breath caught as warmth rose to her cheeks, but she mustered a tiny smile. "Do you think my soul is in need of saving, sir?"

A lazy smile warmed his features in reply. "I won't be drawn into that kind of discussion at the supper table. But I will ask if you'd care to take a walk with me when we finish, as I assume the parlor will be busy—if that's acceptable to you and our hostess."

Julia dipped her head. "I am agreeable, if Katherine doesn't have other plans."

It appeared Katherine had caught at least the last part of their conversation. "I have no other plans, but the children can use the upstairs parlor, and Micah and I will be cleaning the kitchen, so please feel free to stay in the downstairs parlor. I can't imagine it will be too noisy or busy."

The table quieted as she spoke. Mr. Tucker set his cup of coffee down. "I had already decided to work in my room this evening, so I'll not be in the way."

Beth shot a glance at her aunt and a tiny smile peeked out. "Aunt Wilma and I are taking a walk, so I believe the parlor will be quite empty."

Frances leaned back and crossed her arms. "That leaves me. I suppose I can clear out, as well, so you two can have some time alone, although it would be more proper if you had a chaperone."

Julia wasn't sure what to say. It appeared the entire house was conspiring to leave her and Seth alone in the parlor. She looked his way, but he sat still, his face unreadable.

Wilma raised her hands in disbelief. "I declare, Frances Cooper! Leave it to you to be blunt as always."

Frances snorted. "I always say, a person should speak their mind and be honest when needed, and I do not see that it is necessary to prevaricate, in this particular instance."

Wilma huffed. "I believe Pastor Seth and Miss McKenzie are fine left alone in a public room for a few moments without your presence as chaperone. And if your ankles aren't bothering you, why not walk with us? We'd be happy to have you."

"Humph. I dare say it would not make you happy, but I appreciate the offer, regardless. I think I shall stay and help Katherine and Micah with the dishes, if it will not offend your feelings."

"I am not so easily offended, Frances, and you know it. Maybe we should all stay and help clean up?"

Katherine's rich chuckle broke through. "Nonsense. The children will clear the table before they go upstairs to read or play games, and Micah, Mama and I can take care of the rest. Go enjoy your walk. Julia and Seth may use the parlor in complete peace, until you return."

Julia's insides shivered. Alone with Seth? But what would she say to him after last night? She wanted to share the decisions she'd made, but she didn't know why he'd come or if he was upset.

Maybe she should claim a headache and go to her room, instead—but that would be the coward's way out. She must see this through, come what may—and pray that what came wouldn't be too painful.

Chapter Nine

Seth followed Julia to the parlor with his body on fire one minute, then shaking as though with the ague the next. He'd been so certain that talking was the right decision, but what in the world was he going to say?

Would it sound pompous or self-serving to tell her that God had opened his eyes to the plight of the Chinese people in this town? She might think he was saying it to get back into her good graces.

Had she ever truly cared about his opinion, even when they were seeing one another so many years ago? He'd thought so back then, and he'd seen recent glimpses of what he thought was genuine interest in renewing a relationship—then at other times, he wasn't so sure. Why did women have to be so complicated?

He paused at the threshold to the parlor as Julia entered, hoping to calm his racing heart and gather his thoughts. The peace of this dimly lit room washed over him, as memories of laughter and the compassion of friends pushed to the fore.

The oversized roll-top desk against the far wall was absent its usual occupant, since Jeffery had chosen to work in his room tonight.

The three easy chairs and long divan draped with cozy knitted comforters and throw pillows enticed him forward, and his feet sank into the plush throw rug, a somewhat new addition that added color to the already attractive room. Julia took a seat in one of the wing-back chairs, and he chose its closest mate.

Julia stroked the crocheted arm cover. "It's so lovely in here. You can certainly see a woman's touch."

Seth's breathing eased at the neutral topic she'd chosen. "Yes. Is this the first time you've been here?"

She nodded, her blue eyes alight. "The ladies invited me earlier, but I never felt comfortable coming." Her face clouded. "Not after some of the things that happened at the church."

"Ah, yes. Mrs. Evans and her ilk." Pastor or not, he couldn't keep the disdain from his voice.

"Forgive me, I shouldn't speak of anyone in that manner, but I know what a trial she can be to anyone she dislikes." He snapped his lips together, appalled that he'd brought attention to Mrs. Evans' dislike of Julia. "I didn't mean it like that. I'm sorry."

Julia gave a wry smile. "It's all right. I know she doesn't approve of me, and probably with good reason. I don't meet her standards of what a proper Christian ought to act like."

He leaned forward and clasped his hands between his knees. "About that, Julia. I have something I'd like to share."

She held up a hand. "Would you let me go first, Seth?"

He considered her request for a moment. "I feel it's very important I tell you what's on my heart, if you'll allow me?"

With a slow nod, she leaned back in her chair. "All right. Go ahead."

Now that she'd agreed, Seth's tongue felt like it had been lassoed and roped to a stout tree, with no way of escape. What had he planned to say when he'd blundered in here?

He cleared his throat, struggling to remember. "Ah, yes. Well now, there's something I'd like to share."

She nodded but didn't speak.

Seth grappled to find the words, thankful this rarely happened when behind the pulpit on Sunday, or he'd be out of a job.

"Because of you, I've realized I've missed part of my calling. All this time I've been in Baker City, I've focused on the people of my church, as well as those within the community that I felt I could help or reach. Never once did it occur to me to go into the saloons or Chinatown."

He uttered a soft groan. "I guess I haven't been much of a shepherd, if I've only noticed the sheep that aren't hurting."

He met her intent gaze. "I know I told you last night that I was going to try to do more, but it never really hit me how little I've done, until I went home, unable to sleep. I can understand why you've been angry with me and other Christians in general. I hope you can forgive me, Julia."

Julia sat frozen in her chair, not sure she'd heard Seth correctly. His confession wasn't what she'd expected. More censure, possibly—renewed efforts to convince her to stay out of the dangerous areas of town—certainly—but a humble apology? It took her breath away.

"I'm not sure what to say, Seth, other than there's nothing to forgive. At least not on my part towards you."

She gripped her hands in her lap, struggling to continue. "I had a wonderful talk with Mrs. Roberts today—about a lot of things. She helped me face my own bitterness, and the fact that I've been holding onto a lot of resentment, which has kept me from forgiving people from my past who hurt me."

Seth sat perfectly still, seeming to almost quit breathing. "Was I one of those who hurt you?"

"Oh, goodness, no. If anything, I realized I must ask your forgiveness for leaving the way I did. It wasn't fair to you—to us, but I was so immature and still trying to find my way. I was afraid to fall in love—afraid that love would tie me down. I wanted time to spread my wings and not be handed from my father straight to a husband."

She bit her lip and looked away. "But I'm beginning to understand that's not the case—it may have been then, but not now."

Sucking in a quick breath, she continued. "I also need to ask you to forgive me for wrongly judging you since I arrived. I put all Christians in the same basket, believing none of them truly cared about the abused in society, but God, through Mrs. Roberts, showed me how wrong I've been. I spent time in my room alone with my Bible today, searching God's word, and I discovered a lot in there about forgiving and being forgiven."

She looked at him squarely. "I let the past go and gave it all to God. Now I must ask you to forgive me, as well." She let her air out in a soft whoosh, keeping a close eye on Seth's face to try to gauge his reaction.

Seth rose and took one step to her, and then knelt beside her chair. He clasped her hand in his and stroked his thumb across her knuckles, sending a delightful shiver all the way to her toes.

"My dear Julia, there is nothing to forgive. All these years, I tried to convince myself it was better that you'd left—that somehow God wanted me to live the remainder of my life alone, but now I know that's not true. I still care for you, and I wonder if you'd give me—give us—another chance? Might I start calling and court you, the way we began seven years ago, and see where it leads?"

Julia could barely concentrate on Seth's words as his fingers against her skin continued to send shivers of delight through her. She gave a shaky laugh and tried to focus. He wanted to court her. He still cared. Complete delight overcame her, and she sighed, wishing he'd kiss her—when a terrible thought intruded. "Mrs. Evans."

Seth dropped her hand as though he'd been burned. "I beg your pardon? Why would you bring that woman into this?"

Julia laced her fingers together, knowing if he touched her again she'd be too weak to resist. "Because she is a prominent member of your congregation, and I don't see how we could court or have any kind of relationship with her disapproval. She's already poisoned at least two other women against me."

Seth reared back. "I don't care what she thinks. It's not her business what we do."

Julia gave a sad smile. "Having been raised in a pastor's family, I must disagree. It is important what she, and the rest of your congregation think. You've established yourself here, Seth. Your people love and trust you. You've built a wonderful church family, and I have no right to come along and destroy that, or at the least, to bring discord or division."

She hunched a shoulder. "I'm sorry. As much as I'd love to be courted by you, I won't come between you and your people. God will have to change their hearts."

She leaned forward and placed a brief, tender kiss on his lips. "And we'll pray that He does. If not, I'll have no choice but to leave Baker City, no matter how much it hurts, for I can't continue to be around you and not want more."

Chapter Ten

It had been two weeks since Seth had declared himself, and Julia had only seen him at service. He'd stopped by the boardinghouse to call on her twice the first week, but she'd told Katherine she wasn't feeling well and stayed in her room. It wasn't a lie—she was heartsick at what she was putting Seth through, as well as sick to her soul at losing the only man she'd ever loved.

She opened her bureau drawer and removed the trinket box again, then reverently withdrew the tissue-wrapped Forget-Me-Not petals that had started to crumble with all the repeated handling.

She knew she loved Seth—that she'd loved him for years but had convinced herself that her calling was more important than love. Why did the two have to be separate? Another petal crumbled as she touched it, and Julia winced. This is what she'd done to what could have been a glorious life with Seth—broken it into tiny pieces that could never be repaired.

Gently she laid the few intact flowers and the fragments back into the box and closed the lid, then walked to her chair and sank into it. Seth didn't understand that she was doing this for him.

It was the right thing to do. For so many years she'd been selfish, wanting her own way, judging people for not seeing the world the way she saw it, but no more. She would not destroy Seth's calling because she couldn't walk away from her own.

Thick clouds had obscured the sun for the past three days, quite in keeping with her mood, but also trapping her in the house more than she liked with the intermittent showers. Then steady rain had started early this morning and showed no sign of relenting. If only she could get out and take a brisk walk—clear her mind and see if God might give her any other options besides the few she could think of.

She'd toyed with the idea of renouncing her calling and marrying Seth. But after hours of agonizing, she'd come no closer to resolving the problem than the night he'd declared his intentions. There was no hope for it. She couldn't discard what she believed, nor could she destroy Seth's ministry.

People might scoff and say she was being foolish, but she knew better. She'd seen firsthand what one or two gossips could do to a pastor's life, and she wouldn't put the man she loved through that, no matter what he wanted.

If she gave in and allowed him to leave the ministry, he'd resent her in the years to come. She couldn't abide that thought. Better to break it off before their hearts were too deeply entangled.

Julia covered her face and groaned. Too late. Her heart was already so entwined with Seth's that she wasn't sure she'd survive the wrenching pain of losing him again. Now she knew what he must have gone through when she'd walked away the first time. At least she hadn't led him on this time, but that didn't bring much solace.

She surged to her feet and moved over to her basin of water. A few ladies from church had been here the past two hours for tea, visiting with Katherine, Wilma, Mrs. Cooper and Beth, but she had remained in her room.

She'd planned to go to the store and pick up a few things, as she'd promised Mei she'd check on her father again. From what the doctor had reported, the older man had recovered and was ready to return to work, if he still had a job.

But after several hours, the torrential downpour showed no sign of stopping. Katherine had assured her that at least one of the ladies would have room to give her a ride.

If the sky didn't clear in a couple of hours, Micah or Mr. Tucker would fetch her. She pulled her everyday bonnet from a bureau drawer and swung her cape over her shoulders. It wasn't cold, but the rain would drench her to the skin even in the short distance from the porch to the buggy.

More than anything she wanted to stop by the church—to see Seth one more time—but she'd promised herself to stay away.

In fact, if she could do so without causing a stir among the kind people here, she'd skip church altogether. If seeing her in the congregation affected Seth even half as much as seeing him did her, she couldn't imagine how the poor man could preach.

As she opened her bedroom door, she heard women's voices raised in laughter. The front door opened and closed, and Julia slipped to the window. Micah had brought the horse from the barn and hitched the buggy.

Five ladies dashed two at a time through the rain and clambered in. She'd better hurry before the last one or two left, so she didn't miss her ride. Of course, Katherine had promised to ask if anyone could take her and said she would call her before they were ready to leave. No sense in making her come upstairs, as it appeared the party had ended.

She buttoned her cloak up to her neck, wishing for the hundredth time she could take a long walk, then headed downstairs.

As she rounded the final corner into the parlor she skidded to a halt and stumbled over the folds of her skirt as a distinct voice came through the open door. But it was too late. She'd stopped just inside the parlor in time to see the smirking face of Mrs. Evans.

The woman looked from Katherine to Julia. "Mrs. Jacobs tells me you need a ride to town, and I am most happy to oblige. I've wanted to talk to you for some time, but you always leave church the second it ends."

Katherine gave a barely perceptible shrug. "I asked all the ladies if they could take an extra passenger, and Mrs. Evans was the only one who came alone. The other buggy was full." She clutched the sides of her skirt in fisted hands, her anxiety clear to see.

Julia wanted to tell the old biddy she wouldn't even think of riding in her buggy then turn and walk back to her room, but something stopped her. She'd spent time in her Bible again, working through more scriptures on love and forgiveness.

Was it possible God placed Mrs. Evans in her path because he expected her to love this unlovable woman, as well? She shuddered and tried to push the idea away, but it persisted.

Mrs. Evans crossed her arms. "Something wrong, Miss McKenzie? Catching a chill perhaps, and you no longer wish a ride to town?"

Julia straightened her carriage and forced a smile, hoping to at least reassure Katherine. "Not at all. I appreciate the offer. I'm ready to go, if you are?"

Mrs. Evans had the grace to appear flummoxed. "Well. I declare. I didn't expect . . ." She waved a beefy hand. "Be that as it may, my buggy is tied to the hitching rail in front, so yes, I'm ready. I'm glad to see you are sensibly attired, but as hard as it's raining we'll still probably get wet."

She narrowed her eyes. "What is so important in town that you can't wait for a better day?"

"I have a few errands to run and items to purchase. If you can drop me at the mercantile, I'd be appreciative."

Reaching for the door, Julia smiled again at Katherine. "If this hasn't stopped in a couple of hours, I'd be grateful for that ride home we discussed."

Katherine touched Julia's sleeve. "You're sure you want to go? Maybe you should wait for a . . ." She cast a quick glance at Mrs. Evans. "For a better day."

"I'd rather not, but thank you." She pulled open the door and sucked in her breath at the amount of water running off the roof. "Here goes."

Picking up her skirt to avoid as much mud as possible, she dashed for the buggy just feet away from the base of the porch steps. Even though the horse had only been out of the barn for a matter of minutes, she was already soaked.

Mrs. Evans followed close behind, and Julia was amazed at how quickly the portly woman bolted up the step and into the covered, two-seated surrey. "It's gotten worse since I arrived. If I'd known this was coming, I would have stayed home."

She picked up the reins and released the brake. "I'm glad Mr. Jacobs untied the horse. At least I didn't have to worry over that."

Julia tried to keep her tone light and cheerful. "And we can be grateful the wind isn't blowing. I'm sure we'll be damp before we arrive, but it's not cold at all."

"Humph." Mrs. Evans shook the reins and clucked to the mare, her face grim. "Move along, Maisy. I want to get home."

As the horse turned the buggy in a half circle and headed the few blocks to town, Julia tried to relax. Maybe Mrs. Evans didn't have a hidden agenda in agreeing to take her along. She should credit the woman with at least a little human kindness.

They moved at a good clip, and Mrs. Evans relaxed her tense posture. "I've wanted to tell you something, and I don't believe anyone else has had the gumption to speak, so I shall." She turned to peer at Julia and raised her brows.

Here it comes. Julia held back a sigh. If she hadn't felt so strongly that she was supposed to try to love and forgive this woman, she'd get out of this buggy immediately and walk, deluge or no.

As it was, she might as well jump in with both feet and get it over with, as the woman seemed determined to speak her piece, regardless. "Yes, Mrs. Evans?"

"I've never seen the need to beat around the bush. Honesty is the best policy, so they say, and I agree. Since it appears our pastor isn't going to set things straight on his own behalf, I guess it's my place."

Julia bit her tongue, all thought of love and forgiveness fleeing like a rabbit before a screaming hawk. "Pastor Russell is an adult, Mrs. Evans. I see no reason why you need to stand up for him."

"Obviously you don't. That's because *you* are the problem. I've seen the way he looks at you lately, and it's sinful, that's what it is! You are not suitable as a pastor's wife, the way you gallivant around with those Chinese."

"Gallivant?" She drew in a sharp breath and exhaled it. "How dare you! Do you have any idea at all what those people put up with at the hands of decent, God-fearing people like you? They need someone who cares, who will watch out for their well-being." Julia was ready to give the woman another piece of her mind when unease hit. Who was she to judge this woman, or anyone else?

"I wish you understood what these people go through, Mrs. Evans. I don't believe you'd be so harsh if you could see into their hearts. They're good, decent folks, and as Christians, it's our place to care for them. Can't you see that even a little?"

Mrs. Evans snorted and shook her reins. "All I can see is that I'm getting wet and need to get home."

Seth roused from his deep study in the tiny church office. He'd worked on his sermon for the first couple hours of the day but couldn't seem to focus and stick with the task. Visions of Julia slipping out of church as soon as the service ended last Sunday still rankled. All because of Mrs. Evans. He had a good mind to sit that woman down and give her a good talking to.

A loud shout in the street intensified to the point where Seth lunged from his chair and raced to the door. Had someone died or was a building on fire? Surely not a fire in this dreadful downpour.

Three men he recognized from his congregation ran past the church heading toward the river, and a small group of Chinese men followed behind.

He moved to the top step and cupped his hands around his mouth. "What's wrong?"

One of the men who attended his church slowed and turned. "River's rising fast. Must be from the heavy melt off in the mountains with all this rain. Don't think the bridge is gonna hold." He jerked a thumb toward the bridge in the distance then dashed off again.

Seth reached inside the door and grabbed his coat, then hesitated. What if the bridge gave way and someone was on it? He ran back inside and rummaged in a storage closet where they kept all sorts of tools and supplies.

Yes. A length of rope at least one-hundred feet, once used to secure a man while working on the steep church roof. He slung the loop over his arm and ran, praying the bridge would hold, and if it didn't, that no one would be hurt. Surely there would be plenty of warning for anyone crossing before the high water reached it?

More people streamed past, all running the same direction, voices raised and arms waving. No one seemed to care about the fact they were getting soaked to the skin. He lifted his eyes to the sky. It seemed to have slacked off a bit. Just a steady rain now, instead of a deluge. He rounded the final corner and the river came into sight, with the bridge only a hundred feet away. Seth skidded to a halt and tried to take in the wall of water roaring down the ever-widening channel, taking out small trees and brush along the edge.

Right then, the rain slowed to a drizzle, and in the distance a cloud parted and a weak ray of sun broke through.

Breaking into a jog, he directed his attention to the bridge and sighed in relief. A fast-moving wagon appeared to have cleared the structure seconds earlier and reached the side closest to town.

Seth looked more closely as he got within thirty feet. A small surrey pulled by one horse could be seen barely past the mid-way point. A woman passenger pointed at the water, and her high-pitched scream smote his soul like a dagger.

He sucked in a deep breath. "Julia! Mrs. Evans! Get the buggy off the bridge. Fast!" He sprinted, praying he'd get there in time, praying the horse would somehow reach the other side before the water struck.

Julia gripped the side-rail of the surrey while Mrs. Evans stared at the river and shook. The older woman held the reins but failed to urge the nervous horse onward.

Julia grabbed Mrs. Evans and shook her. Still no response. Julia snatched the reins and reached for the whip perched in the nearby stock. She raised it above the mare's hip and screamed at the top of her lungs. "Yah!"

The mare's already distended nostrils flared wider, and she bolted forward.

Relief flooded Seth. The surrey was within twenty feet of the bank. They were going to make it!

Julia had never experienced true terror—bile rose in her throat, but she pushed it down. It was up to her to get them to safety. Mrs. Evans appeared as though she might faint at any moment and was totally useless. "Hold on. Only another fifteen feet or so." She gritted her teeth and smacked the terrified horse again.

A wave that looked like the fist of a giant smashed into the side rail of the bridge, sending a wall of water cascading over the floor and sweeping the mare off her feet. The surrey stayed upright for one heart-stopping moment, then the traces broke, the reins ripped out of Julia's grasp, and the mare ran free.

The water receded and the mare cleared the last few feet in a wild bound, leaving the surrey teetering on two wheels.

Water swamped the surrey again at the same time a loud splintering noise reached Julia's ears. A broken wheel or the bridge giving way? She didn't know. All she could do at the moment was hold on and pray.

Chapter Eleven

Julia wrapped one arm around Mrs. Evans and clung to the handrail of the surrey with the other, as the conveyance went over on its side.

A man's voice shouted her name. Seth stood only yards away, teetering on the bank and acting as though he might leap through the water to come to her aid.

Julia felt another blast of water and was pulled under, losing her grip on Mrs. Evans. Her mouth filled, and her heavy skirts dragged her toward the bottom of a dark abyss.

She tore at her skirt, ripping the buttons that held it closed and kicked the heavy thing off, not caring that she only wore a chemise, cotton petticoats, and bloomers beneath. Right now survival was more important than modesty.

Kicking with all her might, she surged to the surface, breaking through and gasping for air. The current had sent her toward the shore, but where was Mrs. Evans?

She struck out, thankful she'd somehow broken free of the raging current. Somehow she must make it the last few yards before another wave struck.

Something smacked her arm, and she pushed it away, certain a branch or tree would suck her under again.

"Julia!" Seth's voice boomed from nearby. "Grab the rope."

She stopped struggling and tried to get her bearings as the current increased its pace. Seth must have raced ahead of her down the river. He'd waded out to his ankles and held a coil of rope. He lifted it high and threw it again, as she passed where he stood.

She coughed out another mouthful of muddy water and grabbed for the line, snagging it in time.

"Hold on. Don't let go. I'll pull you toward me." Seth gave a gentle tug to make sure he didn't pull it from her grasp. When she appeared to have a firm hold, he waded out as the water rose past his ankles, praying he could keep his balance.

Fear gripped him in a vise so tight he thought he'd choke to death. Never had he experienced such terror as when he'd seen Julia go over the side and disappear under the water.

Carefully, slowly, he drew the precious burden clinging to the rope toward him. Once he got his arms around that dear woman, he was never going to let go. Another wave swamped her, closing over her head and almost stopping his heart.

If he released the rope and plunged out to get her, he could miss and never get another chance. "Julia, can you hear me?"

She rose to the surface, sputtering and coughing. He stretched as far as he could without stepping into the raging current that could sweep both of them away.

"You're almost here, my darling. Hold on a little longer." Five more feet. Four.

He reached out and clasped her arms, drawing her to him, then walked backwards until he found firm footing. Finally, he tossed the rope over his shoulder, then stooped down, gathering Julia into his arms.

He plucked her from the water and cradled her against his chest, not caring that his trousers were soaked and he was disheveled. "Are you all right? Are you hurt? Can you talk? If only someone else had seen me run down here to find you, but they stayed with the surrey and Mrs. Evans."

She pressed her face against him and choked out another mouthful of water, then slipped her arms around his neck. "My throat is sore from swallowing water, and I'm shaky, but I'll be fine. Put me down, Seth. I can walk."

"Not until we're out of this water." He plunged forward, slogging through the mud covering what used to be beautiful green grass.

Julia slipped from his grasp as soon as he'd cleared the debris field. She placed her palms against his cheeks. "Oh, Seth. Thank you isn't enough! I don't know what to say."

He leaned down and kissed her gently, then tucked a long lock of wet auburn hair behind her ear. Intense love and gratitude swelled in his heart. "As long as you're safe, that's all that matters."

Julia looked up into his warm, comforting eyes, wishing she could feel his lips on hers again. Then she gasped and pulled out of his arms, turning toward the river. "Mrs. Evans! Where is Mrs. Evans! Oh my heavens, Seth. What if she drowned?"

Another spasm of coughing wracked her body, and she bent double. Finally, she dragged in a shallow breath and faced him, her legs shaking so hard she could barely stand. "We were arguing when the water hit us. Neither of us was paying attention, and we didn't see the danger until it was too late."

She felt sick to her stomach and had all she could do not to sink to the ground. "If she dies, it will be my fault. If I hadn't allowed myself to get angry at something she said, we might have seen the water coming and gotten across in time. She was rude, but I lost my temper and said some things I shouldn't."

"It's not your fault, Julia. I heard you scream and saw where you were when the water hit the bridge. You couldn't have made it across."

He took her hand. "But let's go back upstream and see if she's been found. I ran quite a distance following you, and most of the people stayed when they saw the surrey go into the river. I didn't pay attention to anything else."

He plucked his long coat off the bank where he must have tossed it. "Take this. I don't want you to catch your death from being drenched." He wrapped it tenderly around her, helping her slip her arms inside. It fell well below her knees and added to her burden, but at least she was covered and warmer.

Visions of Mrs. Evans' terrified face filled Julia's mind. The woman had been frozen in fear, unable to move when she'd seen the danger. Julia had been able to remove her heavy skirt and strike out for the shore, but would Mrs. Evans have been able to do so?

She didn't even care that she didn't have her outer garments on, and doubted anyone would notice, now that Seth had loaned her his coat. Right now all that mattered was discovering what had happened to the older woman.

Julia gripped Seth's hand, gathered the coat and her soggy petticoats and limped along on shaking legs, hoping her strength would hold up.

Seth prayed all the way back to the bridge that Mrs. Evans was safe, but he couldn't help wondering what the woman had said that upset Julia so. It wasn't like Julia to lose her temper with a stranger—but then, Mrs. Evans could provoke a lamb to anger without even trying.

They passed a group of men attempting to hold the spooked mare, dragging the harness behind her as she plunged across the clearing. Seth stopped and inquired along the way if anyone had seen the driver, with no result.

Finally, a man nodded and pointed a distance away. "Over that'a way. Heard tell some Chinamen pulled her out. Doc's with her now. Pretty sure she's alive."

Seth glanced at Julia, and all the air whooshed out of his lungs. "That's good! The doctor wouldn't be checking her out if she wasn't alive."

Julia nodded, but her face remained grim. "I need to see for myself. Please, Seth, will you take me?"

"Certainly, and I pray she's all right, but are you sure you shouldn't go home and change? A doctor needs to check you out in case you were injured and don't realize it yet. I can stay and see to Mrs. Evans."

She shook her head. "I'm not going to get back to the boardinghouse soon, anyway, with the damage to the bridge." She pointed that direction. "It seems the river took out a section, and I doubt it will be safe to cross until it's fixed."

"I agree. We may be able to do something to help Mrs. Evans or the doctor, in any case."

Julia hurried along beside him, and he slowed his step so she could keep up. His clothing was almost as soaked as hers, but he imagined it must be difficult to navigate in her heavy, wet skirts.

She clutched his arm, and he heard a soft intake of breath. "Seth. Mei Lee and Meng are there, along with their father and some of the other men from their community. Do you think they were the ones who rescued Mrs. Evans?"

Several white men and women stood on the fringes of the group, but the Chinese men had formed a semi-circle around the prostrate form, the doctor and the Lee family. Seth stopped at the doctor's side as he recognized the older man who'd attended Mr. Lee a couple of weeks earlier. Mei's father was drenched, as were Mei and two other men. Even young Meng was wet to his waist, but his face wore a beaming smile.

Mrs. Evans lay on her side, her chest heaving and rasping coughs pummeling her body, as water trickled out between her parted lips. Her face was as pale as bread dough, and if it hadn't been for the wheezing, Seth would have thought she were dead.

Seth touched the doctor's shoulder. "How is she, Doc? Mrs. Evans attends my church. Will she make it?"

"It appears so. I think we've worked most of the water out of her lungs, and she's coming to now. Does anyone have a blanket?" He peered around at the crowd.

A Chinese woman stepped forward, her head down, but she held out a clean woolen blanket.

The doctor took it and nodded his thanks. "Pastor Russell, would you lift her and we'll wrap this around her?"

Seth carefully lifted the older woman who looked at him with a glazed expression. "Pastor Russell?" She gasped out the words and coughed again. "Did you save me?"

Seth leaned closer to the ailing woman, noticing that Julia had hung back and was whispering with Mei Lee. "No, but don't try to talk. We'll get you to the doctor's office where he can care for you properly."

She reached out and clutched his arm. "Miss McKenzie. Died? Drowned? My fault. I couldn't move. She tried to save me." Another spasm of coughing racked her body, and the doctor tucked the blanket tighter around her heaving shoulders.

Julia had been anxious to speak to Mei Lee and discover what had happened. She spent a couple of minutes in whispered consultation with the younger woman before Seth spoke her name. He beckoned to Julia, and she came forward, squeezing Mei's hand. "Speak to her, Julia. She's beside herself with worry."

Guilt warred with irritation and compassion in Julia's heart as she leaned over the cantankerous older woman—a woman who had done her best to put Julia in her place and separate her from the man she loved.

She realized now—after almost dying—she loved Seth with every fiber of her being. She didn't want to love or forgive Mrs. Evans, but the fear and guilt she'd experienced when she believed the woman had drowned came back full force.

Julia didn't release Mei but knelt beside Mrs. Evans and drew the young woman down with her. "I'm alive, Mrs. Evans. I didn't drown, and it wasn't your fault."

Sobs broke out, and the bedraggled woman moaned and shook so hard Julia thought she'd break a bone. "Shh . . . it's all right. Everything is all right. You're reacting to the terrible scare you had, but you're safe now."

"But it *was* my fault! I was so busy telling you what you were doing wrong that I didn't see the flood coming."

Her body continued to shake, and her voice rose in a wail. "You saved me! I felt your arm around me. You kept me above water until something dragged me from your grip. How did you find me again and pull me from the river?"

Julia smoothed the muddy, tangled locks off Mrs. Evans' forehead, all irritation and guilt swept away by concern and compassion. "I didn't find you or pull you out. I almost drowned as well, but Pastor Seth saved me."

"Did he save me too?" She batted tear-filled eyes at Seth. "I'm so sorry I've been angry with you, Pastor! You could as easily have let me drown."

She rolled her head from side to side and moaned. "What are all these other people doing here? Why did you bring all these Chinamen?"

Some of Julia's compassion withered, and she frowned. "These Chinamen saved your life, Mrs. Evans. Not Pastor Seth, or I, or any of the townspeople. Lee Mei, one of her friends, and her father, who has only recently recovered from a serious wound, jumped into the river as the current dragged you under for the third time."

She worked to keep the anger out of her tone. "They had ropes tied around their waists, and some of the other men held onto them, but it was extremely dangerous, just the same. When I spoke to Mei, she told me an uprooted tree barely missed killing her father as he reached you. Somehow he got the rope off himself and around you, and these other men . . ." she motioned at the cluster of silent Chinese behind them, "pulled you in. Mei was able to hang onto her father or he would have perished in the heavy current."

Seth edged closer and put his arm around Julia. "So you see, Mrs. Evans. Had it not been for these brave, noble people, you would have died."

Mrs. Evans' mouth hung open, and a gurgling noise emanated from her lips, but the words were unintelligible. Finally, she coughed again, looking wildly from Julia to Mei and back again. "But . . . but . . ."

Julia pushed back the edge of the blanket and grasped the struggling woman's fingers. "There are no buts, Mrs. Evans. You were saved by these people from certain death. You owe them your life."

Slowly, she nodded. "I see. I had no idea. I didn't realize . . ." She choked on what sounded like a sob and then started to cough again as a nearby wagon rolled to a stop.

The doctor waved at the two men who jumped from the seat. "Bring the litter along with more blankets. Pick her up gently and get her covered, and take her to her home. I'll ride in the back with her and make sure she's all right."

He stood and moved to the side as the men brought the canvas litter suspended between two long poles and laid it next to his patient.

Julia walked beside the litter until the men slid it into the back of the wagon, then she leaned over the wooden side. "Don't worry, Mrs. Evans. You're going to be fine after a few days, and Mei Lee, her father and the other gentleman will all be fine, as well."

Mrs. Evans' watery eyes brimmed with tears that trickled down her damp cheeks. "Were they hurt on my account? I'm so sorry." Sobs tore from her throat.

The doctor climbed in beside her, and the driver clambered onto the seat. "That will be enough now, I think."

The doctor patted his patient's arm. "You need to rest and not think about anything other than getting well. You can thank these fine folks in a few days, if you don't mind them stopping by to see you, that is?"

Mrs. Evans groaned. "I don't mind at all. Thank you, doctor. And Miss McKenzie, I hope you'll forgive me . . ." Sobs obliterated the rest of her sentence and coughs wracked her body.

Julia stepped back into Seth's warm embrace as the wagon jolted forward. She lifted her voice over the creak of the harness and snorting of the horses. "I'll come by to see you, as well, when you're up to it."

Seth drew her close. "That was very good of you. Many people wouldn't have forgiven the way she's treated you."

Julia shook her head. "I've been forgiven much, and I can do no less for her." She raised her face and found her lips only inches from Seth's. "I think I should probably find some dry clothes, now, and go back to the hotel."

She wished she could stop the warmth from creeping into her cheeks, suddenly remembering her lack of attire, bedraggled hair and the stench that rose from her wet clothing. What must Seth think of her?

He placed his fingers under her chin and tilted her face up again. Slowly, he held her there, and his lips quirked in a slight smile. "You appear like you need to be kissed, Miss McKenzie. I'm thinking it might warm you up."

"Seth!" She gasped and tried to pull back, mortified that someone would see or hear, but his grip around her tightened.

"I'm warm enough with your coat." The words tumbled out on their own, when what she longed to do was beg him to follow through on his offer. Surely he wouldn't—not out in public, with him a pastor and all.

He came closer until she could feel his light breath on her cheek. "You might not be cold, but I could certainly use some warming up. I think this might do the trick." Something akin to a wicked grin touched the corners of his mouth as he leaned closer.

"But what will people think?" She barely whispered the words, wondering why she continued to argue when she so desperately wanted his kiss.

"I don't care what they think. And if the expressions of any of our friends are an indication, I believe they agree with my sentiments completely."

"Seth! But you can't ..." The last words were silenced as his lips covered hers with a sweetness Julia hadn't known could exist. They lingered for several long moments, tenderly moving against hers, and bringing all sorts of unknown sensations to the surface.

Finally, when he withdrew a couple of inches, she sucked in a soft breath. "Oh. My. Goodness. That was . . . amazing."

His grin *was* decidedly wicked this time—something she never thought she'd see on a pastor's face. "Want to do it again?"

She struggled in his arms, making him break his hold. As much as she'd love a repeat of that performance, she couldn't imagine what people were thinking—or saying. She glanced around, relieved, but most of the remaining bystanders had wandered away, probably after the wagon left and the excitement died down—not realizing the town pastor was going to offer a little excitement of his own.

However, Mei and Meng stood off to the side giggling, then they dropped their heads. "Seth, we need to go. I've got to get out of these clothes and see if there's a room at the hotel. It could be days or longer before the bridge is fixed and I can get home."

Seth smirked. "Oh no you don't—you aren't getting away that easily. While you were talking to Mrs. Evans in the wagon, I gave Mei Lee some money. I asked her to go to the mercantile and buy what you need. She'll bring it to the hotel where I'll get you a room—at least long enough for you to get a bath, a nap, and change your clothes."

"Oh?" Julia fervently wished no one was around. She was half tempted to give him a kiss or two of her own, she was so giddy with excitement and the joy of being alive. "And why, may I ask, would I only want to stay part of a day?"

Seth kept his arm around her and with his other one, he swept her off her feet and cradled her close. "Because before this day is over, I intend to make you Mrs. Seth Russell. I told you when I pulled you out of that river, that I'm not letting you out of my sight again."

He tipped his head and gave her a gentle kiss. "You've had too many close calls as Julia McKenzie, and from now on, I'm making it my business to keep you safe. Besides, since you can't go to the boardinghouse, and I have a very nice parsonage that's too lonely and big for a single man, I think it's the perfect solution."

Julia's heart tripped like a child playing the drums for the first time—joyous and completely out of control. She lifted her face, no longer caring who noticed.

"You are a very wise man, Pastor Russell. I think I have to agree that's the perfect solution, but . . ." She raised her brows and assumed a gruff demeanor. "I want to be asked, not told."

His smile faded, and he slowly set her on her feet. "Forgive me, my darling. Of course you do. I love you. I think I've always loved you, from the first moment I saw you. I'm not sure how I survived all these years without you . . ."

She placed her fingers over his lips and grinned. "That's perfect, Seth. Actually, all you really need to do to get your way is to kiss me again. Then you can marry me, and I'll expect a few dozen of those kisses a day, to make up for all the years we wasted."

Chapter Twelve

Julia drew in a long breath, wondering if she'd made the wrong decision. But there was no help for it now—she'd sent word to Mrs. Evans that she planned to visit this afternoon.

She had convinced Seth they needed to wait a couple of days before they married, to allow her a chance to rest and get ready. In the meantime, they had visited the older woman's home once in the past twenty-four hours, but this time Julia came alone.

Not quite alone—with this 'little warrior' by her side. She smiled and squeezed the small hand that gripped hers so fiercely "Are you ready to go see the lady you helped save, Meng?"

He turned an expectant face up to hers and broke into a wide grin. "Meng ready to do anything Miss Ju-la want."

Her heart swelled with love for the child. She rapped on the door, praying their reception would be kind. Hopefully she hadn't made a terrible mistake by not warning Mrs. Evans of her extra visitor.

A young woman close to Julia's age stood in the doorway, nodding and smiling. "Mrs. Evans is expecting you." She peered down at Meng, and her lips stretched wider still. "What a lovely child."

Meng straightened his thin frame. "I not lovely. I fierce. My name Meng, not lovely."

The young lady bit her lip, and her brown eyes danced with merriment. "Pardon me, Meng. I can see you are very fierce, indeed."

She opened the door wider. "I'm Martha Waters, and I live next door. I came over to check on Mrs. Evans, and she asked me to see you to her drawing room. I've laid out the tea, but she tires easily after her ordeal, so please try to keep your visit brief."

Julia nodded. "Thank you, Miss Waters. We won't stay long."

They followed her to the open archway leading into the drawing room and hesitated as Miss Waters departed. Should Julia announce them or simply walk in?

"Don't stand out there gawking, Miss McKenzie. Come in. I've been waiting for you to get here." Mrs. Evans' querulous voice smote Julia's ears, and she cringed.

Gripping Meng's fingers tighter, Julia marched into the room, determined to get this errand over and praying it would have the desired effect.

Mrs. Evans peered at her, then lowered her gaze to Meng and gaped. "Why did you bring that child here, Miss McKenzie? I was under the impression you were coming alone, since Pastor Seth was unavailable."

Julia stopped in front of the divan across from where Mrs. Evans sat, her feet propped on a hassock and a knitted throw on her lap. "I thought you'd want to meet the little boy who helped save your life."

Mrs. Evans leaned forward and squinted. "Why, he's a tiny mite of a thing. He's barely big enough to pick up my teapot. I do not believe for a moment he could have helped pull me from the water."

Meng slipped from Julia's grip and glowered. "I strong. I no baby. Meng help Poppa and Mei and others get you out of the water. Miss Ju-la not tell lie." He crossed his arms over his scrawny chest and stared. "Why you say that, anyway?"

Mrs. Evans stared at the boy, her lips parted, and only a gurgling sound coming from her mouth. Finally, she choked and gasped, then spoke. "I do declare. The boy has spunk! I like children with spunk." She extended her arm. "Come here, child."

He stepped forward but didn't relax his stance.

She bit her lip and snorted a laugh. "So you helped get me out of that river, did you?"

"Yes. Meng very strong."

Mrs. Evans peered at Julia. "Is that why you brought him to see me?"

Julia plunged forward, sensing this might be the right moment. "He's alone all day, Mrs. Evans. His sister and father work, and his grandmother is old and deaf. As you can see, he's not getting enough to eat, and I fear for his health. Plus, although he speaks passable English, his sister has a burning desire to see the boy better himself."

"And what are you hoping I might do about it? I'm not a tutor or an English teacher."

Julia's heart sank. "Yes, ma'am. I hoped . . . I know you have strong feelings about his people, but after what they did for you, I assumed you'd want to help. But I certainly won't impose on you further." She reached for Meng's hand.

"We need to go home now, Meng. Mrs. Evans is tired and must rest." The boy caught hold, and she drew him toward her, knowing he'd understood most of what she'd said and hating that it might have hurt him.

"Hold on now. I didn't ask you to go." Mrs. Evans threw off the coverlet from her lap and reared forward, almost tumbling from her chair.

"This boy needs fattening up. He's much too thin. And I may not be a teacher, but I think I speak English quite well. In fact, I pride myself on my elocution and precise diction. I imagine I could do something with him, if that's what you're asking."

Meng scowled again and stomped his foot. "I not too thin. I strong. I not eat lady's food. She mean. I not like mean people. I help save lady, and she not say thank you to Meng. She need to be polite like Miss Ju-la."

He tugged Julia toward the door. "Go home now. Eat scraps. No worry, Miss Ju-la. Scraps fine for Meng."

Mrs. Evans gasped and fanned herself. "Oh my word. The child in incorrigible." She took a step forward. "Meng, I must ask your pardon. I did not know I was being . . . mean."

A scarlet wave crept up into her cheeks. "You are too bold and outspoken for a child, but I do want to thank you for helping to save me. Will you stay and have tea and cake with me?"

Meng stared without speaking for a full minute, then slowly nodded. "Yes. I stay and eat cake. Miss Ju-la stay too. Then we talk about English."

He plunked down in the middle of the divan and grinned. "Meng like cake. Maybe Mrs. Evans not too mean for Meng to stay and eat a piece."

Seth's hands shook as he tugged at his closely tailored sack suit jacket, then adjusted his four-in-hand tie. Somehow he'd allowed Julia to talk him into waiting two days to marry, but denying her anything at this juncture wasn't possible.

Besides, she'd been exhausted from her ordeal in the river, and it hadn't been fair to press her, no matter how anxious he was to make her his bride.

He hoped the surprise he'd planned for this afternoon would please her. They were marrying at his church and had decided not to spread the word. People were still cleaning up from the recent destruction, and Julia didn't feel up to making a large production of the affair.

Time to go—he could hardly wait to see her again. Seth walked out the door of his house, thrilled to think that the next time he stepped over the threshold it would be with his bride in his arms.

He'd never dared to hope Julia would have him, but now that dream would become a reality.

The sun shone bright on his face, adding even more warmth and joy to his day. The mud had dried in all but the deepest ruts in the road where wagons kept it churned up. Normally he enjoyed walking almost anywhere he chose to go, but today was different. This occasion called for his horse and buggy. He wouldn't take a chance of Julia soiling whatever dress she had chosen.

Seth stopped beside his horse tied to the rail and stroked the gelding's face. "Thank you for being so patient. It took a little longer to get presentable than I expected. Do you think Julia will like what she sees?"

He moved backward a step and grinned, then walked to the buggy and climbed up. "Come on, old boy, let's get to the hotel before she thinks I've forgotten."

He caught a glimpse of the river in the distance through the grove of trees and worked to suppress a shudder as the memory of Julia's near miss smote him. How different things would be now if he hadn't been able to reach her in time.

As he guided his horse around a particularly muddy patch, he prayed that the message he'd sent by boat to Micah had made it in time.

The bridge wouldn't be repaired for at least another couple of days, but Julia and he were concerned the folks at the boardinghouse would worry themselves sick about her safety when she hadn't returned.

A group of men had put together a raft, and this morning was the first time they'd made a trip across. Seth had urged Julia to rest and prepare for their simple ceremony and not think about riding the raft, and she'd agreed, as long as he'd send a message to their friends.

Both foot and wagon traffic had resumed, and Baker City appeared to have returned to normal operation. Men, women and children lined the boardwalks, appearing to enjoy the welcome sunshine and eager to get out after the extended downpour.

He pulled his gelding to a stop in front of the Arlington Hotel, set the brake, wrapped the reins around the handle, and climbed down, his heart nearly pounding out of his chest.

Seth tied his horse to the rail and turned, hesitating a moment. Would Julia be waiting in the lobby, or would he need to send word to her room? Standing here wouldn't accomplish anything. He grinned and bounded onto the boardwalk then made his way into the lobby.

Butterflies danced in Julia's stomach, and she felt almost giddy with happiness. She'd purchased a new dress yesterday, as well as picking up a few other necessary items. The past two days she'd rested well and felt completely recovered from her ordeal in the river. Even her visit with Mrs. Evans yesterday hadn't dimmed her joy.

In fact, if anything, the woman had added to it, as she'd offered her thanks once again and spoken a blessing on Julia and Seth's coming union—not to mention the alteration in her manner toward Meng.

By the time they'd finished their tea and cake, the little boy's attitude had changed. He'd wormed his way into the older woman's heart, in spite of the wall she'd tried to erect.

She peeked out the window, looking for Seth. Should she stay in her room and wait for word or go to the lobby? Pulling out her little watch for the third time in an hour, she grimaced. Seth wouldn't arrive for another fifteen minutes, unless he was more anxious than she. How had she survived all the years they'd been apart, much less not realized her love for this wonderful man?

She couldn't abide sitting in this room another minute. At least in the lobby she'd be surrounded by people and time would pass faster.

Drawing in a deep breath, she worked to compose herself, knowing she'd see Seth soon. She wished some of her friends could attend today, but she was content with a simple ceremony overseen by the Episcopal pastor.

As soon as she stepped into the lobby she looked at the front door—just in time to see Seth enter. What would he think of her ivory gown with the puffy sleeves and v-inset that accentuated her waist? She couldn't believe her good fortune when she'd found it at the well-stocked mercantile yesterday.

Seth's lips formed an 'O', then a gentle smile tugged at his mouth as he moved toward her. "I've never seen you so lovely." He took her hands and drew her toward him, stopping before public propriety would be offended.

Julia's breath stuttered at the joy in Seth's eyes—pure devotion shone there for anyone to see. "Thank you, Seth."

She tried, but no other words would move past the lump in her throat. She'd never thought it possible to be so happy.

Seth took her shawl from her arm and draped it around her. "I believe the pastor is awaiting us at the church. Are you ready?" He quirked a brow at her and smiled.

"Completely." Julia breathed the word as joy blossomed in her heart.

Ten minutes later, he helped her down from the buggy as close to the church steps as possible. She wondered at the wagon and buggy parked nearby. The pastor might have driven rather than walked, but who else would be here?

Seth held the door open and waited for her to enter then slipped in beside her, his arm settling around her waist. He leaned close and whispered in her ear. "I hope you don't mind?"

Several heads turned and then a number of people stood from the pews at the front of the sanctuary—Katherine and Micah Jacobs, Mrs. Roberts and Beth, Mrs. Cooper, and the children, Lucy, Amanda and Zachary.

Julia gasped and put her fingers to her lips. And Mrs. Evans. The older woman was the last person she expected to see here.

Seth smiled and tightened his grip. "Are you happy? You don't mind that I asked them to come?"

"Mind?" She faced him and her hands crept up to his lapels. "Only one other person would make my joy complete. But I understand why you couldn't invite her to your church, Seth. Truly I do."

He cupped her cheek, and his thumb stroked her skin, sending delicious shivers up her spine. "Only one? I would have thought at least three."

His smile widened, and he dipped his head and touched his lips to hers. "This is only the first of the things I've planned for our future that I hope will make you happy, my darling."

Releasing his hold, Seth pivoted and motioned toward a side door where the women's quilt group sometimes met. "You can come out now."

Mei, Meng, and their father tiptoed into the room. Julia hesitated only a second, then she dashed forward and embraced her friend.

"I can't believe you're here! Thank you for coming. Mei, I want you to stand beside me when I marry Seth. Will you do that, please?"

Mei brightened and then clapped her hands. "I do it with much joy. And Mrs. Evans, she agree to teach little brother while Mei at work. Mr. Seth, he get my father a job cleaning the church and tending the cemetery. He no longer have to work at the mine."

She turned to Seth as a tear crested her bottom lashes. "Oh, Seth."

He nodded and moved forward. "You're crying? Why…?"

She giggled. "I'm not crying. I'm in heaven right now. You are the most amazing man I've ever known."

Seth's smile returned. "That's not all. Mei, did you bring the gift I asked you to find?"

She nodded and turned, then disappeared into the room and returned holding a cluster of blue Forget-Me-Not flowers tied at the base of their short stems with a white ribbon.

"These for you. Pastor Seth ask me to find. Meng and I pick them on a hillside. Pastor say they your favorite flowers."

Meng nodded, his eyes bright. "Miss Ju-la, I help, too." His scrawny chest seemed to swell. "You like?"

She took the bouquet. "Yes, Meng. I like. In fact, I love them. Thank you." Her gaze swept the front of the sanctuary and encompassed silent but grinning faces.

"Having you all here makes my joy complete. After all these years of trying to find something that was missing, I've rediscovered my lost love and found a new family."

She turned to Seth and placed her hands on each side of his face, then rose on her tiptoes to give him a light kiss. "My heart has finally come home at last."

Author Notes

One of the most common questions asked of an author is, why did you write this book? What prompted the story? Two things come to mind with *Forget Me Not*. The first was the interest that Pastor Seth generated in book one in the *Love Blossoms in Oregon* series, *Blowing on Dandelions*.

Readers were impressed by his compassion toward Micah Jacobs when tragedy hit and they wanted to hear more about him. That got me to thinking—where had Seth come from, and why was he still single at the age of twenty-eight.

In the 19th century, most men that age were married with a family well under way. It's always fun for an author to satisfy the questions and interest of readers, and this story was no exception.

I truly enjoyed digging into Seth's past and discovering why there was no special lady in his life—only to find there had been at one time, and she planned to make an appearance soon!

While doing ongoing research during the writing of book three, *Dreaming on Daisies*, I discovered something else that I hadn't realized during the writing of the first two novels. There was a section of Baker City called Chinatown.

When we visited there a couple of years ago, I saw the remains of a Chinese cemetery, with most of the remains removed to China or other family plots over the years. As I continued my research, I found that the Chinese population was an integral part of not only the mining industry, but the coming railroad and the town.

In fact, there was one thing that really impressed me. The business owners in town, on the whole, treated the Chinese decently. Many of the men came to the United States alone, leaving their families behind in China and sending money home, or eventually, when they saved enough, bringing them to join them.

History records that the Chinese Exclusion Act of 1882 restricted most Chinese entry into the United States. The law was a reaction to the influx of Chinese workers, especially in the West, where thousands worked for lower wages in mining, ditch-digging, and railroad construction.

A number of Chinese men had returned home to bring their families back, but couldn't return without a sponsor. Several businessmen in Baker City sponsored these men and their families, allowing them entry back into the US.

Beginning in its early days, Baker City had a Chinatown located between Resort Street and the Powder River. Chinatown included several businesses, a Chinese temple, private dwellings, opium dens, and prostitution cribs.

What I discovered about the people piqued my interest and curiosity, and stirred the question author's often ask . . . what if? What if a white woman who cared about the plight of the Chinese women who worked as prostitutes came to town—and to complicate things further, what if she had once been in love with the local pastor?

And so Julia McKenzie was born and came to reside in Baker City, where her old flame, Seth Russell, had established residence a few years before.

It's evident that *Forget Me Not* comes after book one, *Blowing on Dandelions*, since we see that Katherine and Micah are married, but nothing else is given away. By the time I decided to write *Forget Me Not*, I'd already completed and turned in all three books in the series—and book two, *Wishing on Buttercups* was close to release—too late to make any changes.

Pastor Seth is shown very little in book three, *Dreaming on Daisies*, but as it hasn't gone through line edits yet, I may go back and add mention of Julia when or wherever Seth is shown so the reader knows Julia exists.

I'm considering another novella using Mei as the main character, and a secondary character you'll meet in *Dreaming on Daisies* as the hero.

I hope you've enjoyed whatever part of the series you've read so far. If this is your first meeting of the folks in Baker City, be sure you go back and pick up a copy of *Blowing on Dandelions*, so you'll find out how Seth intervened in Micah's life and get to know the residents of the boardinghouse a bit better—I believe you'll be glad you did!

*My Facebook Fan Page:
https://www.facebook.com/ MiraleeFerrell

*Twitter: https://twitter.com/#!/MiraleeFerrell

*My personal website: **www.miraleeferrell.com**

View pictures of my book research and travels, family photos, upcoming speaking event updates (via my blog link), and find announcements about future books. Also, click on my blog link to read updated posts and sign up for my newsletter.

You can also drop me a note at **miraleef@gmail.com**

41736185R00092

Made in the USA
Charleston, SC
10 May 2015